World Stage Press
Verse from the Village

MY FATHER'S SON

Katherine and Jonathan's story

A NOVEL

BY RENEE CHATMAN

World Stage Press

Verse from the Village

World Stage Press
Verse from the Village

My Father's Son
© 2018 Renee Chatman
ISBN-13: 978-0692172322
ISBN-10: 0692172327

First Edition, 2018

Printed in the United States of America

Cover Design: Camari Carter-Hawkins
Back Cover Design: Emi Hasegawa
Edited By: Marilyn Forrest and Camari Carter-Hawkins
Layout Design: Emily Anne Evans

This book is dedicated to all the characters that take up space in my head fighting for their stories to be told. This book is dedicated to my children; Amber, Nia, Lonnie Jr. , Jehlali, and Debenaubi, who were there when I first gave these characters their voice.

TABLE OF CONTENTS

FOREWORD

The subject of race in America is not as complicated as some purport it to be. On the contrary, I believe the subject of race in America to be very simple. The difficulty lies, not in our ability to understand our past, but in our current agreement to avoid collectively summoning the courage to deal with who and what we were. I believe our agreement not to look back in a courageous way is what leads to the belief that things are 'complicated.'

At the time of this writing, I am a 50-year-old black man living in America. Growing up watching my parents; survive day to day for a time in Chicago; watching their frustration after a long vacation drive on the road as they tried to get a hotel for the family in Boston (black face value rejection after blackface rejection); Hearing how their navigations of corporate friendships at the office with certain 'understandings' in place (of course) and then listening as they came home to make drinks and vent loudly in the living room. And then me, personally, feeling the 'metaphorical' whip of hearing the 'N' word all through the schoolyard and on the way home; enduring fist fight after fist fight. Surprisingly amidst all of this, I was never made to feel a victim. I have memories of a wonderful childhood. Why? Because my childhood wasn't in black and white. It was in color. Bad people had layers to them. Good people had layers to them. I knew when and where to be to enjoy myself. I stood far enough away from the villains so that I could watch and learn why they were the way they were.

It would have been easy for this wonderful novel, by Renee Chatman to fall in line with the current ongoing editorial of historical American white people 'bad', historical American black people 'victim', but that might be a limited narrative for the listening ear at this point. Oh make no mistake, evil was and still is evil, but to truly go back in time and look at what our racial history is, I deem it infinitely more courageous to climb into the skin of our 'bad' and the skin of our 'victim' and allow ourselves to be surprised by new understandings.

This novel brilliantly straddles the consciousness of then and now. In this era of purges, (ME TOO MOVEMENT, POST OBAMA RACIAL AWARENESS), it's quite hard to look back in our country's recent past without instantly demonizing the unbearably vicious actions of those who viewed themselves superior to their fellow human. But to experience Renee's courage as a writer daring to step viscerally in and out of black and white skins in her narrative, blessing us with the gift of UNDERSTANDING, allowing us to see where these painful actions and reactions are sourced. Renee allows us to see ourselves in the 'villain' and the 'victim'. We walk through shifting points of view in this novel and remain stunned by our ability to see the other side of what would seem to be a one-sided debate. And underneath it all, she invites a surprise element; the unerring human capacity to see color where others can only see black and white.

In my opinion, understanding is the gift this novel offers our ongoing national race discussion. No, the blows are not softened because of this. No, the agenda is not to change your understanding of right and wrong. Broadening our capacity to see ourselves in the darkest actions of others is the gift I walk away from most honoring from this work. And that's a healing on many levels for me. I wish you the reader, the same effect.

Michael Phillip Edwards

J. R's Seat

As I sat behind the bus driver, I felt a warm sense of nostalgia wash over me. I have sat in this same seat for most of my bus riding life - right behind the driver, James William Robertson, my father. The route he drove had been his route for over three decades. Stepping onto his bus almost felt like stepping back in time; the smell of the oily vinyl seats, the ding of the bell when passengers pulled the cord to signal their stop, it was all so beautifully familiar. The intermingling of sweat and frustration always lingered in the air as folks piled on and off the bus. Always at just the right time, the small cassette tape player would come out of nowhere and fill the bus with the soothing sounds of the O'Jays' classics, "Back Stabbers" or "Family Reunion." This let everybody know, they were on James William Robertson's bus. Relax and enjoy the ride. The bus always felt like home.

Looking at my father drive, it was obvious this was home for him as well. He knew every twist and turn of this route, and he knew the names and faces of the people who always rode with him, day in and day out. Recently, my father had reduced his driving time to morning and rush hour only. My mother insisted he needed to slow down. My father knew how important morning connections were for his riders and he wanted to be sure they made it to their connections. Folks needed to get to work on time.

Some of the riders on his route no longer worked at all but would continue to ride along with my father. Getting on at their regular stops, and riding to the end of his route, they would all meet up for breakfast at the small eatery my father owned with my mother and Aunt. It was a very sociable group who had known me my whole life. I rode along with

1

them this morning to join them for breakfast. I guess at any time I could have shaken things up and sat in another seat, but why would I? The seat behind the driver was my seat; JR's seat. I loved sitting behind the magical man. It was always safe. I needed to feel safe right now.

As I leaned my head back on the tattered vinyl seat, I closed my eyes and allowed the noise to fade into the background. Later on, that day I would be heading to the airport to catch a flight to a place I've never been, to meet relatives I never knew I had, to settle the estate of the man whose DNA I shared - a man I had only recently come to truly know, the man I was named after, Jonathan Wallace Richardson. As I sat with my eyes closed in silence, trying to wrap my mind around the new information of my birth, I replayed the story my mother told me in its entirety just six weeks ago. It was the story of her life with Jonathan, and why she left him, to recreate her life, and mine, with the only father I have known.

CHAPTER 1

The Bus Ride

Thirty-two years earlier...1977

The mornings at the Richardson house were always filled with anxiety. My name is Katherine. As the busy working mother of an 18-month-old son, I loathed the time between when I tucked JR in at night, and when I dropped him off at daycare the next morning. Anything could happen between that time, and usually did. This particular morning, I hurriedly dressed myself and the baby before I tip-toed toward the kitchen to get the last cup of milk I had saved for JR's breakfast. My husband, Jonathan, laid passed out beneath the patchwork quilt on an old flea market couch in our small apartment living room. Even passed out, I could smell the nauseating mixture of vodka and vomit on his breath.

Once in the kitchen, I searched the refrigerator for the small cup I had hidden behind the jar of mustard and hot peppers. Dammit!!! It was gone! Nothing was off limits to my husband when he went rummaging after a long night of drinking. Since that was most nights, hiding food became an essential part of our survival. Sometimes I succeeded; today I did not. I began to look around the worn but tidy kitchen to see if there was anything that Jonathan had overlooked that could possibly feed my baby. That was when I heard JR fussing in the bedroom. Poor child was hungry. I hurried past the couch to get to him before he could wake his father. I just wanted to get out of the house on time. Entering the bedroom, my heart almost stopped. Jonathan was holding JR giving him kisses and hugs. In most families this is normal father behavior, but for me, seeing my baby in his father's arms sent a shiver of panic down my spine. When did he get up?

"Where is my son's breakfast?" Jonathan bellowed.

"I was in the kitchen getting it when I heard him crying. I just came to make sure he didn't wake you up."

I stepped forward to take the baby out of Jonathan's grasp, but he stepped back.

"Well you can see I have him. Go get his food. I'll feed him."

I could really smell the vodka on Jonathan's breath. My stomach rose up to my throat.

"Actually, we are out of milk, so I was going to..."

Before I could finish my sentence, I felt the sharp sting of my husband's closed fist. I fell to the floor holding my left eye. Jonathan towered over me.

"You are the most worthless bitch! You are beyond stupid! You ain't as smart at that fancy college piece of paper makes you think you are! Even I know, without a degree, that you need to have food in this house to feed my kid! Why are you working at that fancy newspaper if you can't take care of your responsibilities at home?"

Jonathan continued his barrage of insults, yelling and spitting close to my face. As I held my throbbing left eye, I tried to stay out of his reach. I kept my right eye on JR. All I could think about was how I was going to get my baby out of his arms. Whenever Jonathan woke up before he sobered up, I never knew if I was going to be his punching bag to absorb his anger and pain, or his listening ear to absorb his hurt and disappointment. He never directed his aggression towards JR, but sometimes my poor baby would get caught in the crossfire. One time Jonathan hit me so hard, while I was holding the baby, that I dropped him. He had a knot on his head that I was able to explain away as toddler mishaps, but I didn't want my baby in the middle of any of Jonathan's dysfunction.

While in the middle of his tirade, he grabbed the top of my hair. I was preparing myself to be dragged across the room when, suddenly, Jonathan pushed JR into my arms and ran to the bathroom. The sound of gagging and wet heaving filled the small apartment. His head was still in the toilet when I ran past the bathroom. I grabbed my purse and keys and diaper bag and ran out without looking back.

Holding JR tight, I ran down the street toward the bus stop. I didn't want to be late. The last thing I needed this morning was to have to walk past the full office with sunglasses on to get to my desk. I didn't want to have to come up with another excuse, to another coworker... about another bruise inflicted on me... by my husband. Being already at my desk, deep in work, always fended people off.

I made it down the block and was rounding the corner, hoping against all hope that my regular bus driver was running a few minutes late. I turned the corner, saw the bus, and saw the warm friendly face of James Robertson waiting at the stop. He wasn't supposed to wait like that. It would throw him off his schedule, not to mention the schedule of the other passengers trying to make other bus connections. I was so glad he waited.

James was always smiling. He had the kind of eternal joy I envied. He appeared to really enjoy life. He seemed to really enjoy his job. He knew most of his regulars by name, which included me and JR. If he didn't know your name, he knew your face and what stop you got on and off at. My stop, to drop JR off at child care, was at the end of his route. I was often one of the last people to get off the bus. On good days, we would talk and enjoy pleasant conversation about almost anything. James would pull out his old cassette player and play the same O'Jays tape over and over again. We would laugh and tell each other jokes all the way to the end of the route. On bad days, we would ride in silence. I would catch him staring at us in his rear-view mirror. His eyes would scan us with concern and I could tell he was trying to piece our story together in his head. He would never ask me any questions. He would simply accept my silence and drive his route. At our departing stop, he would always tell me to take care of myself and 'little man'.

Today was one of those bad days. I quickly put on my dark sunglasses and climbed onto the bus. I showed him my bus pass and sat down just to the right of him, where I always sat. James watched me settle into my seat.

"Good morning Miss Katherine. Glad you and little man could join us this fine day."

"Thank you, James."

I kept my head down as I adjusted JR on my lap. A tall older black man yelled from the back of the bus.

"Hey driver, can we get going? Some of us have to get to work on time!"

He was wearing what looked like a mechanics uniform. He was named Ted Charles, a regular on this route.

"Now Mr. Charles, you know I will get you to your connection on time. I always do, don't I?"

James yelled over his shoulder, looking at Mr. Charles, in his mirror.

"Well, yes you do Mr. Robertson, yes you do."

Mr. Charles started to chuckle to himself and soon the whole bus started to chuckle too. I let out a soft sigh of relief and leaned my head back on my seat. On this bus, I was safe. No yelling husbands or nosey coworkers. The left side of my face ached. I knew my left eye was starting to swell and change color. I closed both eyes and listened to the casual banter of my fellow passengers allowing their conversations to take me away from the real stress of my real life.

James rode his route, engaging in his usual ribbing and joking with his regulars. Mrs. Folks worked at a flower shop, three days out of the week. Her husband had recently retired from his job with the city sanitation department, with a really good pension. She didn't need to work, but if she couldn't find a reason to get out of the house for a couple of hours, he was going to drive her crazy. Mr. Nguyen was a soft-spoken Vietnamese man who was a cook at the "Soul Shake" soul food restaurant. His wife, a petite caramel colored black woman, was as loud as Mr. Nguyen was quiet. She was a nurse at an old folks' home. She tried to act like Mr. Nguyen's flirting bothered her, but we all knew better. I was half listening to everyone's conversations and half letting my brain float away, when I felt JR stir in my arms.

He said. "Mommy, hungry!"

Fuck! I still hadn't given him something to eat. I hated to send him to daycare on an empty stomach. I had no cash on me. Jonathan had found that too. Maybe I would have time to go to the bank and write a small check before I dropped him off. I could get him something then.

"Mommy's sorry, baby boy. I will get you something as soon as we get off the bus."

I cooed into my baby's ear. "Mommy promises."

I started to dig through the diaper bag, hoping there would be some Cheerios or Ritz crackers in the bottom that would pacify him for a little while. I was in luck. There was a plastic bag with a handful of Cheerios in it. I handed the bag to JR and watched his little fat fingers attempt to fish out the cereal one by one and shove them into his chubby baby face.

The morning rush started to slow down and the passengers started to thin out on the bus. James took out his O'Jays tape and popped it into the cassette player. The sound of "Back Stabbers" filled the space. James' baritone voice harmonized with the song, as though he was a member of the group. That made my little one smile. That made me smile. We were at the second to the last stop. He let off his last customer. It was only me and JR left. I started to gather my things together. James suddenly pulled off his regular route and stopped in front of a donut shop. He left the door open while he ran inside the shop and up to the counter. From where I sat, I saw a brown-skinned woman, with the same smile as James, meet him at the counter. They spoke for a brief few seconds, then she handed him two bags and a small cup of what I assumed was coffee. As he walked back to the bus, I noticed for the first time how large a man James was. Not only in height, he appeared to be well over six feet five inches, but he was a large man in stature as well; Solid. Strong. His presence filled the doorway as he entered back onto the bus and quickly returned to his route.

We pulled into the station where the drivers sat to change shifts. James was a few minutes ahead of his schedule. He opened the door and then handed me one of the small bags and the cup of coffee.

He said. "I didn't know how you like your coffee, so there is cream and sugar in the bag."

He tore the wrapper off a straw and inserted it into a carton of milk.

"I hope you don't mind if I give this to little man. I thought it would be rude for you and I to be drinking and he not have something too. I also got a plain donut for him, if you don't mind him having it."

Before I could say Yes or No, JR had grabbed the carton and was sucking down the milk.

"Well, I guess that's a Yes then!" We both laughed and James tore off a small piece of the donut to hand to JR, who then shoved the whole thing in his mouth.

"Wow, I'm impressed. How did you know not to give him the whole donut?" I said in amazement as I watched James patiently hand JR a small bit of the donut one piece at a time.

"My sisters all have kids. I have them all the time. Kids will put the whole thing in their mouths if you don't watch them."

James pulled out another carton. This one was chocolate milk. He ripped open the top and guzzled half the carton down. He wiped his mouth with a napkin from the bag. He offered me a buttermilk bar, before taking one out of the bag for himself. We sat in silence, eating, without feeling, when the next driver pulled up to relieve James of his shift.

"Katherine, do you mind if I walk with you to drop little man off at day care?" James asked rather shyly.

"James, I don't want you to go any more out of your way for us. You've done enough already. Thank you so much for the coffee and donuts, but I can take it from here. I'll see you tomorrow morning."

I adjusted the baby on my hip, threw the diaper bag and my purse across my shoulder and headed toward the childcare center at the end of the block. I got maybe halfway there when a beige company car pulled alongside me and rolled down its window. There sat the gentle giant of a man that was James behind the wheel smiling at me.

He said, with the most sunlit smile I had ever seen. "You know, I could drive you to work after we drop little man off."

I looked at my watch. I still had an hour and a half before I had to be at work. At least an hour of that would be on the bus. If I took the ride, I could be there in 20 or 30 minutes. Feeling the pressure of my eye as it continued to swell beneath my dark glasses, I did something I never believed I'd do.

"Thank you, James. I would really appreciate that ride to work."

James had parked and was leaning on the door of the passenger side, when I walked back out from signing JR into day care. He opened my door to let me slide into the seat. We rode, without speaking, for about a mile.

"I have to drop this car off at the station first and pick up my car. I'm not supposed to have anyone in the car with me, so I'm going to drop you off here, at this coffee shop, if you don't mind."

"I don't want to cause you any trouble trying to help me out." We pulled up in front of a cute looking diner and stopped the car. I had been down this street for years and never noticed it here before.

"No trouble at all. It will only take a minute to get my car. Why don't you have another cup of coffee, before I take you to work?"

Before James could even get out of the car, I had already jumped out and headed to the diner's door.

"Okay then, I'll see you in a few minutes." He chuckled in my direction.

I walked inside the quaint, little shop. A waitress, balancing four plates, and carrying a pot of hot coffee, told me to have a seat anywhere I wished to sit. Looking around, I wanted something close to the front so James would see me as he walked in. I picked a booth by a large window so that I could see him walk up to the door.

The moment I had taken my seat, my mind played back the events of my morning. Suddenly, I became very anxious and nervous. What was I doing here? If Jonathan saw me here, like this, with this man, he would kill, seriously, kill me! My thought was to leave James a note and get out. I needed to be on my bus heading to work. Here I was, acting like some school girl on a date. I started looking through my purse for a pen and a scrap of paper, when James overshadowed my table.

"I see you found us a booth. I don't know if my body will fit in a booth." James joked as he tried to squeeze himself into the bench of the booth. As he sat down, I stood up.

"James, this was mighty sweet of you to offer me coffee and a ride. But, I don't think this is appropriate behavior for me. I am a married woman."

Tears started to swell in my eyes, behind the shades. I quickly wiped them away before they fell down my cheeks. James untangled himself from the booth, without saying a word. He gently guided me to a small table near the back of the diner. He motioned for me to sit. I sat. He sat. Out of nowhere, the waitress from earlier, showed up at our table.

"Good morning, James. You having your usual today?" The woman's lovely disposition was contagious. She had skin the color of perfectly polished Maplewood, and a smile that looked just like James'.

"Good morning Charlene. No, won't have time for that this morning. Could you just bring me a cup of hot coffee, for the young lady here, and a large glass of chocolate milk, for me?"James' eyes never left my face.

"Will do." Charlene spun around and was gone. James and I sat in silence.

Charlene soon returned with a cup and a coffeepot. She placed the cup in front of me and poured.

"I'll be right back with your milk, James."

Once she had completely walked away, I slowly picked up the cup and brought it to my lips. I didn't bother to add any cream or sugar. The warmth of the liquid clearing my throat helped to calm my nerves, just a little bit. I kept my head down looking into my cup. I could feel his eyes observing me. He said nothing. Charlene returned with a tall frosty glass of chocolate milk. He took a long drink. I took another sip of the most perfect cup of coffee I had ever tasted. I put my cup down and finally looked up to meet James' stare. He reached across the table to take my hands. I quickly pulled them away and placed them in my lap.

"Katherine, don't you think it's time you tell someone what's going on? If you can't tell me, I understand, but you have to tell someone."

James spoke with a kindness and compassion that I had been missing; longing for. I took another sip of my perfect cup of coffee, as a single tear rolled down my cheek. I didn't bother to wipe it away this time. I put my cup down and removed my sunglasses to reveal the dark purple and blue-black eye they hid. The black eye was courtesy of my husband, Jonathan. James remained quiet. It was time for me to talk.

MY FATHER'S SON

CHAPTER 2

Katherine
(The Last Track Meet)

In order to know how I married a man who could put his fist through my face, I have to start from the beginning. The year of 1967, I was a senior in high school. Not just any high school, but the best high school in town, of which there were three. I grew up in a very small, podunk town in the deep rural Georgia south. The water tower sat on the outskirts of town and brandished the slogan: 'Where your Neighbors are your kin. ' Most folks in our town never left it. You were born there, you lived there, you died there. Everyone knew everyone. I had known Jonathan, my sweetheart, since we were young enough to share the same bath water.

Out of the three high schools we had in our town, two were for the whites, and one for the Negro kids. One of the white schools was named Robert E. Lee High. It was closer to the end of town, where most of the folks, who worked in the factories, lived. The school I went to was Thompson High, the other white school. It was closer to the center of town. Most of the kids I went to school with had parents who ran the town in some way. Either they owned the factories or the bands or had some type of office job. My father worked for the only advertising business in town. Jonathan's father worked for the only bank.

The high school for the Negro kids was named Lincoln High. All of the Negro kids and some poor whites went there. Although everyone knew everybody else, we really didn't know much about those kids. We did know who their families were. The same families had also lived in town for years. Most of the men worked in the tobacco factory, packing and lifting boxes. Most of the women were domestics. They had their own little community near the end of town. It was just a couple of blocks, but they had their own church, elementary school and grocery store. We knew that in other parts of the country and in the big cities, segregation and civil rights were hot topics. Our town had not experienced any of those problems. I would hear the old folks in town often say, "Our coloreds know their place and stay there," and, "Our coloreds are doing just fine and are happy here."

I had never had a full conversation, with a Negro directly, to ask them if they were happy, but I guess it must have been true. Our small town never had any of the uproar, riots and chaos that we were witnessing on the evening news.

On the day of the last track meet of the year, Thompson High would run against the all-Negro team from Lincoln High. Sporting events were the only time we ever mingled with the Negro kids. Some of us tried to invite them to a school dance once, when I was on the junior dance committee. It didn't get much support, so we dropped the idea. Most of their games were played against other Negro schools in neighboring small towns. Our school only met with theirs once, maybe twice, during the season. We never had any idea how good the teams were until we met them on the track.

There was a rumor going around that our coach had gone to watch them practice earlier that week and came back saying that they were as fast as it gets. They were supposed to be unbeatable. An hour before the meet, I was crossing the football field, heading toward the gym. I found myself walking behind the Negro team, as they exited their bus. I couldn't hear the whole conversation, but I could tell it was heated. As I got closer to them, I overheard some of the boys talking to their coach.

A brown-skinned boy, with a lot of thick hair, like cotton candy, said. "I want to beat these boys just one time!" He sounded so angry, almost winded like he had just run a mile.

Another tall and muscular boy, said with a surprisingly soft voice. "I just want to wipe those smug looks off their faces, just once!"

"Now look boys, we don't want any trouble out here with these folks. Willis, you've already gotten your acceptance into college. You don't have anything to prove to these people. Now let's just do this and get home safe and in one piece."

The coach was an older, good looking man. He almost looked like a chocolate Santa clause. I could tell he was trying his best to calm the boys down. Some of the other boys all started to talk at once. I couldn't make out what they were saying.

Someone must have pointed me out, because all of a sudden, the whole group got quiet. Some of the boys moved to the side away from me. I picked up my pace and walked toward the gym. Their conversation started up again as they made their way toward the guest area.

I bounced into the gym looking for the rest of my squad. I was a cheerleader. I was Head Cheerleader, actually. We didn't cheer for track meets but seeing that it was the last meet of the year, we wore our uniforms to show support and school pride. I didn't tell anyone what I had overheard from the Negro boys. We made our way out to the track. It felt like the whole town had come out to watch our boys. Race after race the Negro boys would start out in the lead but would run out of gas just before the finish line.

The crowd watched in collective silence as the last race, the 4x4, was being set. The gun signaled and off they went. As with the other races, the Negro boys were way ahead the whole time. My Jonathan was the anchor. I watched as his hands gripped tight around the baton. I knew he had been working on his technique and I was impressed with his new-found speed. Lane 2 was in the lead. Jonathan was in lane 3. I could see the determination on my Jonathan's face as he fought to catch up to lane 2. I recognized lane 2 as one of the boys I had heard talking earlier. He was the one they called Willis.

Willis looked relaxed. His head was up, and his shoulders were loose and confident. At the last straight away, I saw Jonathan start to catch up and inch past him. The crowd was on their feet. Willis never broke his stride and it almost looked like he was slowing down. A few feet from the finish line, Willis tried to lean in, but it was too late. My Jonathan crossed first. The crown went wild. They were on their feet cheering and whooping it up. We won! The cheerleaders and I headed to the track, just as the crowd rushed the field.

"I thought them boys were supposed to be as good as it gets!" Jonathan laughed with his fellow teammates.

His best friend, Matt said. "I think they just have the other teams scared to really challenge them. That can't scare us!"

Jonathan shielded his eyes from the bright sun and asked. "You think them college scouts were impressed, coach?"

"You did just fine young man. I wouldn't be surprised if the next time we hear from you, it's from one of those fancy colleges up north." The coach shook Jonathans head like it was a basketball. "Ok gentlemen, let's go shake these losers' hands."

"Coach…I ain't shakin no nigger's hand!" the red head boy yelled from off the bench.

"Yes, you will Cody. We have manners on this team. It shows good sportsmanship. Besides, we won! Don't you want to be able to rub that in their faces?"

"Heck yeah!"

All of the boys stood up and formed a line to meet the Negro boys line. The coach shook the Negro coaches hand and said something in his ear that made the Negro coach smile.

Jonathan was standing alone when I caught sight of him. He took off his tank top and used it to wipe the sweat from his face and neck. When he looked up, we made eye contact. He smiled at me. I loved that smile. Almost like the sun came down and kissed him right on the mouth. Unfortunately, I wasn't the only one who noticed his smile. As I moved through the crowd toward Jonathan, I walked behind two of my fellow cheerleaders, Peggy Wilson and her best pal Susan Peterman. I heard Peggy tell Susan that she had plans to meet with Jonathan later on that night. I would have gotten mad if it weren't so funny.

Jonathan Wallace Richardson was many things. He was an athlete. He was the pride of Thompson High's basketball, football and track teams. His outgoing personality and leadership skills made him every guy's friend. His dark looks and tall athletic body didn't hurt his standing with the girls. Not that I had anything to worry about. No matter how many girls threw themselves at him, I knew Jonathan only had two loves. Sports were his second love. I was his first.

"Did you see me, Katie?" he asked me, earnestly.

Jonathan stood 6 feet 3 inches. He was always heads over everyone else. He pushed through the crowd, past Peggy and Susan, and scooped me up in his arms.

"I sure did baby. You were amazing!" I returned the enthusiasm.

"I'm going to hit the showers and get some last minute talking from coach. But meet at my house in an hour. We can go celebrate properly." He planted the sweetest kiss on me, before letting my feet slide back down to the ground. He turned to leave, then turned around again, to give me a wink. I giggled as I watched him back away and get enveloped by the crowd. This was his moment. I was so proud of him. I turned around and almost ran right into Peggy. I didn't know how she ended up behind me.

"Oh Peggy, hi! Great meet, right?" I walked away with a big smile on my face. Without looking back, I could feel the daggers Peggy was throwing at my back. As I walked away, I could hear Susan questioning Peggy about her so-called date with my Jonathan. I'm sure she made up something, to save face.

***

I had time to go home and freshen up before I met Jonathan at his house. The Georgia heat made everything sticky. I wanted to change out of my uniform into something light and cool. I lived just a few blocks from the school. I walked past white picket fences and manicured lawns. Multi-colored flower beds and soft pastel painted houses. Growing up in a small town was all about what life looked like from the curb. Nobody stood out or looked different. As I walked up to my own cookie-cutter, perfect home, and put the key in the door, I wondered if people thought my life was Leave-It-To-Beaver perfect. I wondered what it felt like to have Mrs. Cleaver waiting on the other side with milk and cookies.

My mother, Marian Shelby, was no Mrs. Cleaver. She was an ambitious woman who made her way from teacher to the principal of the local junior high, and head of the school board. The first few years of my life, my mother was a homemaker. Once I entered into first grade, she went to work as a teacher. That was around the time when my father's job as a salesman was slow and we needed the extra income. Daddy's sales picked up, but mother never returned back to homemaking. Daddy didn't mind. As long as my mother was happy doing what she did, Daddy was happy letting her do it.

Of course, having a mother that was a teacher put a lot of pressure on me to be smart and do well in school. My mother was smart, and when I was a small girl, she expected me to be smart too. But something started to happen around the time I got into the 6th grade. I started to develop, physically. By the time I was a freshman in high school, well, I filled out my sweaters without the help of socks like my friends used. That's when Mother started treating my education different.

"Stop asking so many questions in class. The boys won't ask you out if they think you are smarter than they are!" She would scold.

I wasn't really worried about how smart the other boys thought I was. I only had eyes for Jonathan. Even then, he only had eyes for me. In my junior year, Jonathan and I were pinned. Mother was so excited, you would have thought it had happened to her. It was at our senior prom that Jonathan asked me to marry him. Mother was beyond excited and proud. The Richardsons and my mother went way back. My mother and Jonathan's mother, Sandra, were close friends when they were little girls. Back then, her name was Sandra Miller. They went to school together, from kindergarten all the way through high school. They even went away to college together. Mother was the reason Sandra and Edward Richardson even met.

Once Jonathan and I were engaged, my education issues really began. As a teacher, it was her job to stimulate and encourage young minds to learn all that they could. Unfortunately for me, my mother felt that education for girls and women was only so they would be smart enough to catch the right, educated husband. With my marrying into one of the richest families in town, well, I was done learning.

"If a man is to be the head of the household, then he needs to feel that he is the smartest one in the house. He needs to know that the future well-being of the family is for him to figure out." These were some of the things my mother would repeat to me everytime she witnessed me with my girlfriends talking about college.

"...a girl as pretty as you will have no need for college. Your soon-to-be husband is certainly being groomed to take over the family business. Your new life will consist of things you surely could not learn in a college!"

It was overwhelming sometimes. I would hear her in my sleep. I felt like she thought if I were smart, it would ruin my life and my marriage. It was all very confusing. My mother was a very smart woman. She always had been, from as back as elementary school. Some folks say she was a genius, especially when it came to math. Any type of math, Mother would excel in it. Daddy said being that smart was embarrassing to her.

No matter how many times he tried to convince her otherwise, Mother always felt plain and physically awkward. She wanted to be seen as pretty, not smart. Beauty was her tender spot. Sandra Richardson was her idea of the perfect beauty. Mother would go on and on for days for every little thing Mrs. Richardson would do to her hair, or what clothes she wore, or what lipstick she would wear. Whenever Mother would read anything about what Mrs. Richardson did, in the society pages, Daddy and I knew we were gonna be hearing about it for the next week. I, sometimes, suspected that Mother wanted to be Mrs. Sandra Richardson ... be that beautiful, I mean. Maybe she thought that would have given her a better life ... money wise, I mean.

As plain as my mother felt, she still managed to land one of the most handsome men in town. Daddy was a much sought-after bachelor, after graduation. He was tall, well-built and muscular. He had been an athlete in college. He was dark and handsome, with movie star looks. Although Daddy had grown up in the same town, he was still a bit of a mystery to most folks. That made him even more attractive. My parents met when they were both working at a sales firm in town. This was after they had both come back from college. Mother worked in the secretary pool. She said the women would go on and on trying to get Daddy's attention. Imagine their surprise when he fell for Mother. Daddy always said the most beautiful thing about a woman is her mind - the unique way women figure things out and are more often correct. I wished Mother felt that way.

I walked through the door, glad to get home before Mother did. I headed straight to the mailbox to see if the last acceptance letter had arrived. I had applied to five different schools, for Jonathan and myself. We wanted to go to the same school. With us being married, we figured we would get housing. We both wanted out of the small-town life, and away from small town people. So far, I had received four acceptance letters. Jonathan had received four rejections. The last school to respond was the University of Illinois. It was in Chicago. A recruiter had come to the school and seemed very interested in Jonathan for track and basketball. He even met with coach, his teachers, and parents. They had a great journalist program there. That would work out perfect for the both of us. I wanted to become a writer, maybe work at some big city newspaper in New York or Los Angeles. Jonathan wanted to be a track star and run for the USA Olympic track team. After winning his gold medals and breaking world records, he would come back to the States and play basketball for one of those big city teams. Maybe he'd play in New York. This had to work. I shuffled through the mail looking for the letter.

This was my last chance. I had no backup plan if Jonathan didn't get accepted in.

"You looking for this?"

I heard the rich bass of my daddy's voice behind me. I turned around to see him standing in the doorway to the kitchen. He was holding a large envelope in one hand, and what I'm pretty sure was a rum and coke, in the other. Daddy had been a salesman. All my life, as far back as I could remember, that's what he had done. He was good at it, too. Why, when the market was hot, Daddy could sell ice to a snowman.

There were a few lean years. People just didn't have spending money like they used to. That's when Mother went to work as a teacher. Over those next few years, the company Daddy worked for started growing. Daddy was back in the saddle again. He made quite a bit of money for them. The company developed, what they called, an in-house advertising department. They asked Daddy to run it so he didn't have to travel as much as he did before. He had set hours most days. Most of the time, he got home before Mother, like this day.

"So, another college recognizes how smart my baby is!" he said while tossing the envelope around, out of my reach. "Which one are you thinking about choosing?"

"It depends on which one Jonathan wants to go to." I didn't want to tell him that Jonathan had no choice. I wanted him to believe that Jonathan had options. Daddy thought that Jonathan was a dumb jock. Unlike Mother, he thought I could do better.

"Now, look here girl, don't go planning your future around some idiot jock, who don't even know what the inside of a library looks like. You're smarter than that. I don't get what you see in that boy. I know your mother loves him. She thinks he's some kind of golden-boy god, but you, chipmunk? My dear daughter, you could have any boy you choose, why that bonehead?"

Daddy was laughing so hard at that point he barely heard my response to him.

"Daddy! Jonathan is not a bonehead and he's a Richardson. He doesn't have to go to a library. He probably has more books in his family library, than the library has in it, anyway...and he loves me and I love him. Isn't that what's important?"

Daddy stopped laughing long enough to roll the ice around in his glass just before taking another sip of rum and coke.

"Well, I guess it is darling daughter. I know he better treat you like the princess you are!"

I grabbed the envelope out of his hand, kissed him on the cheek and headed toward my room.

"He treats me just fine Daddy!" I yelled over my shoulder just before closing my bedroom door.

I shoved the envelope into a large hat box that held the other envelopes I had received, in the back of my closet. I quickly changed out of my cheerleading uniform into a light floral print sundress that showed off my shoulders. I touched up my face, with some light concealing powder. I grabbed a sweater and headed over to Jonathan's, with my fingers crossed that he had the same envelope waiting for him when he got home.

CHAPTER 3

Jonathan
(Meeting with Father)

Jonathan Wallace Richardson was very excited. The events of the day had his adrenaline on overload. He took a quick shower at the gym and raced home as fast as his '65 Ford Mustang would go, without getting a traffic ticket or in an accident. He pulled up on the lawn in front of his family's large home at the end of a picture-perfect cul-de-sac. A slim man, with skin the color of peanut butter, was working in the yard, when Jonathan drove up to the house. The youthfulness of his face did not reveal the many years he had been working on the Richardson estate. Without saying a word, the older man walked over to the car to take the keys. As Jonathan jumped out of the car, the older man climbed in, to properly park the car.

"Is my father home, Pete?" Jonathan yelled over his shoulder as he raced toward the back of the house.

"Yes Sir, Mr. Jonathan. He's here." The Gardener said back in a calm and quiet tone.

Jonathan calmed himself down, as he walked through the large double doors, which led from the garden, into the large kitchen. Seated at the table, was a brown-skinned woman with a round face, and an even rounder body. She was snapping string beans into a green bowl. Jonathan snuck behind the woman and snatched one of the string beans out of the bowl. That startled the woman. She jumped and looked up from her task.

"Now Mr. Jonathan, you knows better than to put your hands in my bowl whiles I's cooking!" She chuckled and shooed his hand away.

"Hi Josephine, is my mother here?" Jonathan jumped back to avoid Josephine's smacking hand.

"Yes Sir, she in her sittin' room answering some letters."

Jonathan grabbed another string bean and dodged Josephine's hands once again. He walked from the kitchen, into the big, formal dining room. In the center of the room was a long maple table. There were eight high-back chairs around it. Four chairs on two sides. Two armed chairs sat on either side of the China cabinet. The cushions, in the chairs, were a paisley pattern. They were custom made to match the drapes that hung over the wide picture window, on the opposite end of the room. The same paisley pattern covered the velvet wallpaper, which adorned two walls of the room.

In the China cabinet were his mother's prized set of bone China and silverware. They had been given to her on her wedding day. They once belonged to her grandmother. They were a classic pattern that was still available to be purchased. Every anniversary his father would add another piece to the set. This year, he had given her a cream and sugar set. He also replaced a serving bowl he had broken, accidentally, last Easter dinner.

Above the table, a crystal chandelier hung. It held six tiny bulbs that looked like flames. Josephine was instructed to wash each one of them separately. She must have just recently washed them because Jonathan noticed how the sunlight bounced off their glass and lit up the room. He lingered in the dining room for a few minutes to collect himself. His mother didn't like loud noises or too much excitement.

Through the dining room, just left of the living room, there was a small room that housed two wingback floral chairs. A small round table was positioned between them and held a long neck lamp. The shade was covered with the same floral print that covered the chairs. A quaint little writing desk sat between two long thin windows. The pattern on the curtains that hung over them matched the throw pillows that contrasted the pattern of the floral wingback chairs. Behind the desk sat, Sandra Richardson. Sandra was a petite, natural blond, whose figure was well defined despite the plain and simple attire she chose to wear. Her soft apricot complexion was enhanced by the soft, pink lipstick she recently took to wearing. She claimed it was the same color lipstick that Mrs. Jackie Kennedy wore.

"Good afternoon, mother." Jonathan greeted his mother with a gentle kiss on the top of her head.

"You're in an awfully good mood son." Sandra looked up into her son's face.

"Look what I received at the assembly today." Jonathan laid out an assortment of plaques and ribbons he had received earlier that day. "The old man has to take me seriously now. You know they don't just hand these out to everybody. Mother, I even beat the colored boy at the meet today! Nobody beats the colored boys!" Jonathan's voice started to fill with excitement as he relived the day's events for his mother. He saw the anxious look on his mother's face and caught himself. He took a slow breath and quieted his voice down.

"Is Father in his office? I need to show this to him." Jonathan said in a more relaxed tone.

"Yes, your father is in his office, but you know he doesn't like to be disturbed while he's in there. Isn't it enough that I'm proud of you?"

That last sentence was said to an empty room. Jonathan was already on his way down the long hall to his father's office. His excitement felt like it would bubble over. He stopped outside of the office door to again collect himself. After a few brief minutes, Jonathan firmly knocked on the door and waited to be invited in.

MY FATHER'S SON

CHAPTER 4

Edward Richardson...

Edward Michael Richardson was an ominous man. His face wore a full, salt and pepper beard. It was very groomed and neat. His mouth readily fell into a smile that held no trace of joy. An awkward looking man of almost 6′ 5″, he was often overlooking the heads of most men. Despite his height and physical advantage, Edward had no sense of coordination. He often bumped his head on doorways he didn't see coming or tripped and stumbled on small cracks. This was an affliction that had plagued his whole life.

He was born to a single mother, in a working-class area of Atlanta, Georgia. He and his mother were one of the last remaining whites in a rapidly changing neighborhood of Negroes. Edward never knew his father. The little he did know was that his mother's relationship with him caused her to be isolated from the rest of her family. When she found herself pregnant with Edward, she also found herself alone. According to his mother, Edward looked just like his father from the day he was born. He was a large child. Always mistaken for being older than he was, he was expected to behave beyond his actual years.

Edward always knew his mother loved him. In fact, she adored him and did whatever she could to insure his well-being. As a youngster in grade school, he towered head and shoulders above his classmates. He would be the first one picked to play on teams at recess or gym, just to be ridiculed for his lack of athleticism. By junior high, he was already six feet tall, but his inability to excel in sports preceded him every gym period. He, then, became the last kid to be picked, if he was picked at all. He became very withdrawn and shy, trying to shrink himself so as not to be noticed. However, a six-foot white eighth grader was hard to miss amongst a sea of brown faces. The athletes teased him mercilessly, not for being white, but for being so awkward in his body.

He continued to grow. His mother did the best she could to accommodate her son, without the assistance of his father to help her navigate his fast-growing body. She had limited knowledge of sports, so she got him registered for every park sports team she thought would help. When she saw sports were the cause of the decline of her boy's self-esteem, she chose another route. She signed Edward up to every academic program she could get her hands on. To her and his surprise, he excelled, especially in mathematics. Books and numbers became his saving grace. It got him through high school, despite the ribbing from jocks and giggles from girls.

It was his talent in math that got him a full scholarship to Georgia State University, something his struggling mother would never have been able to afford. While he was at Georgia State, he tried to rid himself of the anxiety of being in large groups of people without feeling like everyone was ridiculing him. He joined a few study groups and clubs and started to make a small group of equally awkward friends. It was in one of his study groups that he met Sandra Miller. She was a beauty queen. She was pretty, soft spoken, sweet, and to his surprise, she genuinely seemed to like him. Edward couldn't believe his luck. A girl like Sandra could have had any guy she wanted, and she was interested in him.

Sandra had a college roommate named Marian Tisdale. They were both from a small town a few towns south of Atlanta. Marian was in a couple of his advanced math and accounting classes. He recognized her when she became part of his math study groups. One day while the group was meeting in the campus library, Sandra walked in to meet Marian for lunch. Edward fell in love at first sight. By the end of their freshman year, they were a couple. Before the end of their sophomore year, Sandra dropped out of college. That summer, they got married. By Christmas, Sandra gave birth to a beautiful tow-headed little girl. She was the spitting image of Sandra.

Two years later, sometime during his spring semester, Edward's beloved mother passed. Edward was devastated and unable to make sense of his world. The first woman in his life who truly loved him was gone. Heartbroken, Edward fell into a dark despair that he found hard to climb out of. The thought of knowing he had two people depending on him, helped and overwhelmed him. Sandra had moved back to her small town, with the baby, to be closer to her mother. Without his mother, Atlanta was no longer home for him.

After he graduated, he rode the train back with Marian, to Sandra's small town. This town wasn't like Atlanta. No one in the small town would tease him for being the awkward insecure boy that he still was, on the inside. Edward figured he could reinvent himself and start a new life with his new family. Without the burden of his past, he could stand head to head with everyone else. People would have to appreciate him for being the special talent that he was. He was the man who won the heart of the hometown beauty.

Edward went to work as an accountant in the town's only bank. In just a few short years, he was made the head of the accounting department. He soon discovered he had a real talent for making sound investments. It came as no surprise, in the next few years, when Edward became the youngest bank president and went on to become part owner of the same bank. Yes, Edward had found his place of belonging where he was valued and respected for his mind and his talents, despite his still awkward body. His old, deep-seated insecurities, would rear their unwanted heads time and time again to steal his joy.

Corporate and quarterly meetings would leave him riddled with anxiety whenever he had to stand before a group of people to speak. To calm his nerves and panic attacks, he took to having a gin and tonic before each presentation. Gin was a respectable drink. It was a gentleman's drink. No one knew how much he had begun to depend on it to get through his day of interaction with people. With the aid of the unassuming cocktail, the small town would see Edward as the ultimate professional gentleman. Some folks even thought he should run for office. The drink had a downside to it as well, though, a side his family knew all too well.

CHAPTER 5

Jonathan
(How Smart are You)

Jonathan heard the familiar grumble of his father's voice from behind the wooden door, telling him to come in. The loud scent of lemon oil and old leather, hit his nose the moment he entered the room. His father's office was the opposite of his mother's sitting room. Whereas his mother's space was small and softly decorated in pretty floral and quaint furniture, his father's office looked every bit like a city library, with its floor to ceiling rows of book-filled shelves. Twice the size of his mother's office, it easily accommodated a large hand-crafted mahogany desk, which sat in the middle of the floor, on top of a hand-spun Persian rug. Two large brown leather chairs sat in front of the desk Jonathan's father sat behind. The high-back office chair was made of the same rich brown leather.

His father's back was to him as he entered the room. Jonathan stood between the two chairs, facing the desk, but did not dare sit down before being given permission to do so.

"What brings you to my office today, son?" Edward said, without turning around to look at him. Standing in front of his father, always reverted Jonathan back into a five-year-old boy. His 6'3" frame was no match for his father's overbearing presence. Even though his father was seated, he felt small and insignificant standing there. When Edward finally turned his chair around to face his son, he motioned for him to sit down in one of the fine leather chairs.

Of course, Edward already knew why the boy was there. Reporters from the local newspaper had contacted him earlier to get a quote from the "proud father" of the town's most notable athlete. Edward was far from proud though. In fact, Edward resented his son. He felt like Jonathan was a cruel reminder of the man Edward would never be. His son's athletic abilities came to him so effortlessly. He was gorgeous, thanks to his mother. Nothing about the boy reflected Edward, except for his height and dark complexion. From the time he was very little, Edward watched as Jonathan made friends everywhere he went. People would cluster around him like bees to honey. All of it reminded Edward of all the years he didn't fit in. All the nights he would fantasize of waking up to be one of the beautiful jocks, only to find the same old, awkward him instead. Well if his son was supposed to be the universe laughing in his face, he would have the last laugh. Where were all those beautiful jocks now? None of them had come close to what Edward had accomplished. He worked his butt off in college to make sure he stayed at the top of his class. Then he came to this small town and started from the bottom of the accounting department.

It took him less than 20 years to build his career into something anyone would be proud of. Edward should have been proud of himself, but he was still fighting battles of self-worth in his head. He still desperately wanted to be part of the in-crowd. He felt powerless and judged - never fully feeling like anyone really wanted him in their circle. He knew why people pretended to want to be around him. They either wanted advice on a loan or an investment deal. They never really wanted to just hang out with him. Not as "real" friends. These were the things that were plaguing his thoughts when Jonathan walked through his office doors.

"What is this about, son?" Edward's voice boomed while he looked his son in the eyes.

"Just wanted to show you what I won today!" Jonathan was beaming with pride. His father rarely handed out praises to anyone, including his children, especially not Jonathan. "I wanted to show you the medals I won today. I won big in our final track meet." Jonathan said, still beaming.

Jonathan knew his father hated him, he just didn't know why. He did all that he could to make his father proud, hoping that would satisfy the disappointment. His father had accomplished so much; he thought maybe he wanted Jonathan to do the things he hadn't. So, Jonathan set out to excel in every sport he could. Much to his surprise, he was good at it. He still had to work hard, but when he did, he was always one of the best. From baseball to basketball, football and track, he was a superstar. In his senior year, the coach told him he needed to concentrate on one or two sports so that colleges would come out and look at him. He chose basketball and track. They were his favorites.

Colleges were indeed starting to come around to ask questions about his future academic goals. He knew he had to go to college. His grades were ok thanks to Katie. She was smart like his father. Jonathan figured that once he got into college, his father would see that he was not a disappointment after all. Try as he might, his father was never satisfied with Jonathan simply being good in sports. Jonathan's goal was to be the best. Then his father wouldn't be able to be anything, but proud. His father was a thinker. He was in his head a lot. Jonathan never knew when his father was proud of what he was doing, only when he was disappointed.

Edward sat back in his big chair observing the animated face of his son as he recounted the series of events from the day. Edward gripped the short clear cocktail glass that contained the mixture of his favorite gin and tonic water. He was working on his third drink. He felt a surge of self-righteous empowerment with every gulp of the elixir. His need to rage was beginning to boil to the surface. The slow simmer started two hours earlier while he was on the phone with the lowly reporter assigned to cover the high school sports column.

"Mr. Richardson, I understand you didn't play sports in high school or college. How is that possible? A man with your height must have been a natural. If you didn't play, where do you think your son gets his athletic ability from? It must be nice to see your son achieve things you couldn't." With each probing question and condescending statement, Edward felt his throat constrict, his heart race, and his anger rise. He gave the reporter the response and answers he knew he wanted to hear.

Yes, he was proud of his son. What father wouldn't be? No, he did not play sports, he must have gotten his talent from his mother. She was a cheerleader in high school. He then made an attempt at a joke. "At least one of them knew what to do with this height". Edward gave the appropriate chuckle. Placated, the reporter gave a little chuckle as well, thanked him for his time and hung up the phone. Edward hung up the phone and poured himself his first drink. The conversation that ran through his mind made him more and more enraged.

How dare they make such a big deal out of his son running around like a rat on a wheel in a cage? *It certainly didn't require much brain power to do that. Damn, even niggers could run.* Why weren't the press coming to congratulate him for increasing the quarterly dividends to the banks shareholders, or for approving Jack Olson's loan to save his auto repair shop? Olson didn't even qualify for the loan, based on his lack of business savvy and the low amount of cash he had coming in. It was Edward's instincts that helped him to approve the loan. He had Olson put up the ownership of his shop as collateral. If he forfeited on the loan the bank got the shop. It was in a great location on a main street, in the center of town. With the right business plan, it would be a great investment for the bank. With or without Jack Olson operating it, it was a good investment. His decision saved the jobs of at least 10 people. That should have been newsworthy. He, Edward Michael Richardson, was newsworthy. Instead, they rang his phone to talk to him about his son. Edward's need to be validated and valued was constant. Consistently, he was reminded that his brain mattered little next to the accomplishments of some dumb jock. Even if that dumb jock was his own kid.

"Well Sir, what do you think?" Jonathan's excited, elevated voice broke through Edward's self-absorbed thoughts. He remained sitting back in his large plush office chair staring into his son's flushed face. The voices inside of his head began their debate again. Part of him wanted to look his only son in the eyes and warn him about the real struggles he would have to deal with in the unforgiving world he was about to enter. No matter his athletic prowess, being a player of any sport would not make him successful. He wanted to tell him, that real money would be in owning a sports team not playing for one. He wanted his son to know he was wasting his time running around a track, or trying to throw a ball through a basket. Edward believed his son needed to get his education and his thinking skills in order. It was that same part of him that wanted his son to know that the ability to provide a good life for his wife and children would be more important than any race he would run. It was the part of him that wanted to be a loving father and wanted to give his son a hug and tell him he was proud of what he had accomplished but wanted more for him and for his future.

That was not the part of him who won. It was the angry part of Edward that always overpowered his reactions to Jonathan. For Edward, this man child that was sent to him was a reminder of his own personal weaknesses. The angry part of him felt like, no matter how smart Edward thought he was, the world would still measure manhood in terms of how much physical ability a man had. Edward would be reduced to the little boy who didn't get picked in gym class all over again. The thought fueled his anger and overrode any fatherly feelings Edward may have possessed. Jonathan was the enemy. He was the smug jock in high school that teased him and made his life miserable.

Jonathan watched the familiar shadow fall across his father's face. He was instantly saddened. He was quite familiar with the angry side of his father. As he witnessed the transformation, he prepared himself for the impact he knew would follow. His father's rage rarely showed itself in a physical way, most of the time it would involve a great deal of yelling and berating. But when he drank, the way he drank at that moment, it never turned out good. His father was unpredictable.

"Exactly what is it that you are so proud of, son?"

Within the seconds it took to say those few words, Jonathan's body had its own transformation from 6'3", straight-backed, award winning athlete, to a timid round-shouldered boy, who was afraid to lift his eyes from the floor, refusing to make eye contact with the angry voice.

"Well Sir, coach says I should be able to have my pick of colleges trying to get me to be on their team." Jonathan's once excited voice was now a low whisper.

"Are you sure about that, son?" Edward's voice began to rise.

"Yes Sir." Jonathan said, barely audible.

"You do realize you still need to have the grades to get into college?" Edward's tone was sarcastic.

"Yes Sir." Jonathan kept his eyes focused on the floor.

"So how smart do you think you are? Do you think you're smarter than me?" Edward swirled his drink around in the glass. He took a short sip.

"No Sir, I don't." Jonathan moved forward to the edge of his chair.

"No, you are not smart? Or no, you are not smarter than me?" By now, Edward was screaming across his desk.

Keeping his head down, Jonathan tried to keep his eyes on the cocktail glass in his father's hand. Having emptied it of its content, Edward was still swirling around the remaining ice in the bottom of the glass.

"I would never claim to be smarter than you father." The feeling of his throat closing-in choked off Jonathan's words and threatened to choke off his air. He had the sudden need to go the bathroom.

"So then, son, how do you think you are going to any college?" The intensity in Edward's voice had Jonathan on guard.

"Well Sir, coach says that with my level athletic skills…"

Jonathan didn't get to finish his sentence. The glass that was once in his father's hand, came at him so fast, he was barely able to lean back, stand up and turn his head. He avoided getting hit in the face but couldn't avoid the glass hitting the side of his neck, creating a cut behind his ear.

"Fuck your athletic skills boy! You think because you can run around in a circle, on a damn track, or throw around a fucking ball, that makes you qualified to go to college? Shit, niggers are famous for doing that shit. They probably do it better. Niggers are downright entertaining. What does that say about you, son? Are you saying you're proud to act like a nigger?"

The pain from the impact of the glass left Jonathan feeling dazed and dizzy. He was in pain, but he dared not flinch, or cry, or move, until his father gave him permission. Until he was dismissed, he was not allowed to leave. He remained standing in front of his father's desk, with blood dripping down his neck.

Edward stood up and walked to the front of his large polished desk to look his son in the face.

"Okay son, you believe your sports abilities will get you where you want to go in life? You think you will be able to make a living that can support you and your young bride? Fine, let it then. Let's see how much your physical prowess provides for you, without me propping you up. You will get no money from me!" The heat of Edward's words was just inches from his son's face.

Jonathan kept his eyes staring down at the handcrafted Persian rug that the desk sat on. He focused on the repeating patterns in the design rather than the anger in his face. He was waiting for his father to release him from his tight verbal grip. He felt the pressure in his bladder intensify. The sound of his father's voice became background noise as thoughts of his future came into focus. He was marrying the girl of his dreams in six weeks. And, if everything went as planned, they would get into the same college with full scholarships as far away from Georgia as they could get. He wouldn't need his old man's money. He and Katie would be just fine. The thought made him smile. Separating his future from his present was something Jonathan did whenever he felt powerless to handle a situation. Lost in the thoughts of his future life with Katie, he didn't hear his father tell him to leave his office. Jonathan was jerked back into the room with the rising of his father's voice directly in his ear.

"Son, are you deaf as well as dumb?! Get the hell out of my office!!" The fire in his father's eyes was what Jonathan suspected hell must look like. Hurriedly, he backed out of the room, closing the door behind him.

He quickly ran to the bathroom, located by the laundry room behind the kitchen. He imagined the hard splash of his urine hitting the water was actually hitting his father's face. He immediately felt guilty for having such a thought. Instead of heading back down the hallway toward his mother's sitting room, he headed to the kitchen. Miss Josephine stood in front of a large stove adding cream and butter into a large pot. She looked up when she heard Jonathan walk into the room, but she never stopped cooking.

"Makin' your favorite mash potatoes Mr. Jonathan. I know you'd like that." Josephine saw the blood dripping down the side of Jonathan's neck. She continued to talk about the rest of the meal she was preparing for dinner, as she walked over to the sink and wet a black towel. She pulled a chair away from the table, and gently sat Jonathan down. Slowly, Josephine tended to the cut. The tone of her voice never changed. She made no mention of the wound or the sound of Mr. Richard's yelling that found its way into the kitchen.

"You know I hear you won a whole bunch of honors at your school today. I'm so very proud of you. I know how hard you worked and you deserve all the awards and praises you can get." She patted his cheek and checked her pot on the stove.

"I sho hope you's hungry." Josephine let out a low giggle.

Once she had the cut cleaned up, she lifted his chin so that he looked her in her face. All she could see was the five-year-old-boy who cried when he fell off his big boy bike, the ten-year-old who cried when he fell while trying to climb a tree in the backyard, and the fifteen-year-old who refused to cry when he brought home his first baseball trophy and his father smashed it against the wall. Jonathan had remained very still while Josephine attended to his wounds, physical and emotional. All the sounds around him felt like he was listening with his head in a bowl of Jell-O. As he sat for a while, watching her lips move, the sound started to slowly become clear.

"I cooked up a whole bunch of yo favorite foods. Maybe Miss Sandra will ask your sweet Miss Katherine to join you for dinner."

The mention of Katie's name pulled his head completely out of the Jell-O.

"Is Katie here?"

"Why yes sir Mr. Jonathan. She's in the sittin' room right now sippin' sweet tea with yo mamma."

That was all Jonathan needed to brighten him up. He jumped out of his chair and grabbed Miss Josephine. He kissed her on her cheek before racing out of the kitchen. Jonathan rushed into his mother's little sitting room to find Sandra Richardson still sitting behind her desk, drinking her second glass of sweet tea. Sitting in the floral chair in front of her was Katherine.

MY FATHER'S SON

CHAPTER 6

Katherine
(Hello Mr. Pete)

Walking the five blocks to Jonathan's house revealed a dramatic change in the size and appearance of the houses. My house was on a very nice street filled with identical homes. With the exception of the different flowers in the yard, they all pretty much looked the same - some were two bedrooms, some were three. Our home had three. Daddy bought the house soon after he and mother married. He had hoped to fill it with lots of children. Daddy was an only child. He longed for a large family, of at least three kids. Daddy had it all planned out. He looked forward to having a son. Next, he wanted two pretty little girls. As time went on and mother got older, neither one happened. Daddy thought he had to give up on the dream.

Mother was no spring chicken when they got the news she was pregnant with me. She must have been at least 24 years-old. Most of her peers were working on their second, even third child. I once overheard Mother say to one of her girlfriends, that mothering was not really part of her plans. After she married Daddy, she felt that a wife owed it to her husband to produce at least one off-spring. A man needed to know that his seed was going into the future. That's what mother said. Mother was tickled pink when she found out she was going to the same pediatrician as Sandra Richardson. Doc Michaels was the baby doctor for all the wives of the elite businessmen in our town. At the time, Daddy was just starting to move up and couldn't really afford it. He worked all the over time he could get, so that Mother wouldn't have to go to anyone else.

Mrs. Richardson had already had a baby girl named Julie-Ann, almost five years before. She had also suffered two miscarriages before she became pregnant with Jonathan. I don't know what caused the miscarriages, but from what town gossip said, she had no problem getting pregnant. She would be moving along just fine when suddenly, she would go into labor and lose the baby. The last time she was almost six months along and had to actually go through regular delivery of the child. It was another girl. They named her Martha, after Mr. Richardson's mother. She lived for only 24 hours. They gave her a burial and everything. Poor thing, I couldn't imagine having to go through that. I am just grateful that my Jonathan was determined to get here. He was born a whole three months before me, but we were a part of each other's lives ever since. Mother said it was kismet that Mrs. Richardson had a healthy baby boy and she had a girl. She said it was nature's way of making sure our families would somehow stay supported.

I came to know Mrs. Richardson quite well. I don't know how close they were as children, but I didn't see them behave like close girlfriends. They were more like friendly acquaintances as adults. Most of their interactions were more out of some sort of commitment than friendship. But, Mother was like that with most of her friends.

Three blocks away from home was when there began a noticeable change in style and design in the houses in the neighborhood. The lawns were longer. The houses were larger and farther apart. Most of them were at least two stories tall. By the time I got to Jonathan's block, the houses were a whole house apart. There were only five houses on his entire block. Jonathan's house sat majestically at the end of a cul-de-sac.

On that day, I remember, I walked up the familiar red brick driveway. Jonathan's mustang was perfectly parked at the end of the driveway. You could see it, just as you walked toward the backyard. I saw the gardener, Mr. Pete, cleaning out a flower bed of purple, blue, and pink chrysanthemums and yellow columbines. Mr. Pete had been the Richardson's gardener for a long time. He was a Negro man, small in height. He looked to be around 5'4". He was much older than his thin frame and youthful face would have you think. He never had much to say, but he was always quick with a friendly smile.

I do recall there being another man. He was the gardener, as well as the handyman, who did odd repairs around the house. I would imagine a house as large as it was, would always have something that required repair. He was also Negro, but he was a big man. He was tall and strong looking. At least that's how he appeared to me as a small child. I remember his name was Mr. Otis, and there was a big scandal about him and Mr. Richardson having some kind of argument one night. The following day we discovered the man and his whole family just up and moved out of town in the middle of the night. Mr. Richardson said that the argument was concerning Mrs. Richardson's health. Some say, the Negro man stepped out of his place by making a comment on how Mr. Richardson was taking care of his wife. I remember Mother and Daddy talkin' about it at the dinner table.

"I don't see how Edward is getting away with telling everybody who will listen to his nonsense, that Sandra has 'spells'. Now, Marian, you and I have known Sandra practically our whole lives. We both know she is downright durable. How is it now, she's become so fragile?!"

Daddy never was the type to hold his tongue when he thought something didn't make sense.

"Now Tom," my mother replied, "having miscarriages back to back the way she did could put a real strain on any woman's health, even someone as 'durable' as Sandra."

"Well, I don't claim to know the intricate details of a woman's health, but something just don't seem right in that house to me." Daddy was always a little suspicious of Mr. Richardson. "Tell me baby girl, you seen any funniness going on in that house?"

"...nothing that I have seen, Daddy."

"Now Tom, we don't know what goes on in the private lives of our neighbors. Maybe she isn't as free with sharing her weaknesses to the public. I know I wouldn't be. Besides, how would you feel if someone, working in your home, gave an unsolicited opinion on how you were taking care of me in my hour of need? ...the gardener, of all people!"

My mother believed hired help should never have anything to say to their employer outside of work. She would often give her opinion about the help staying in their place. My mother came from a working-class family, who never were in a position to hire help for anything. We had a cleaning girl once, for a brief time. Daddy dealt with her most of the time. She was often done and gone before Mother even got home. Daddy would hire a handyman every now and again when something needed repair around the house that he couldn't handle. Mother never had to come in real contact with him.

"I don't claim to have known Otis personally, but what I do know is that he was a good man. In fact, I believe I heard it said that he was a deacon in one of the Negro churches." Daddy went on to voice his concerns. "What had to be going on in that house, that was so bad a man like that got himself involved? Something ain't right in that house. Watch what I say. One of these days the truth will come out."

Daddy would repeat his suspicious theory time and time again over the years. He and Mother would go back and forth about the happenings in our small town for hours. Daddy liked to get Mother all fired up in their conversations. They could debate a subject well into the night, the two of them having well thought out positions on just about any topic.

I was thinking about what Jonathan and I would discuss well into the night around the dinner table, as I walked up to the fancy red front door of the Richardson home. Before I knocked, I stopped to talk to Mr. Pete.

"Good evening Mr. Pete." I said cheerfully.

"Good evening to you Miss Shelby." Mr. Pete replied.

"You have this garden looking mighty nice." I stood at the door and looked around the amazing landscape that was the Richardson's front yard.

"Thank you, Miss Shelby, that's nice of you to notice. I's just doin' my job." Mr. Pete lifted his cap and wiped the sweat off his brow.

"Well, it's a good job indeed." I turned to knock on the big red door.

"Thank you again Miss Shelby." Mr. Pete never looked up at me or stopped his workin'. Not once. He kept his head down and kept right on gardening. That was real dedication to the job. I never understood when I heard folks say that Negroes were lazy. From my experience, every Negro I saw, was always working on something.

There was this one time we hired a girl, to help mother out, with the up keeping of the house. I was around fourteen. Mother had just become principal of the junior high. She was trying to juggle her new office duties with her house duties. Something at home was getting the short end of that stick. Dusting, cleaning, and even cooking meals had become harder and harder for her to balance with the demands of her new position at the school.

Mother decided she would just quit, but Daddy wouldn't hear of it. He promised her, he would ask around for a quality part-time cleaning girl. I don't know who recommended her, but I remember the first day Daddy brought the girl to our house. Her name was Tommy-Mae. The first few times she came to the house, I didn't even know she was a Negro. Her skin was the same color as mine. Her hair was the same color as mine, although it was curlier and longer. She rarely spoke and when she did it was really soft. She was shy around everyone, but Daddy. Daddy said she was working to save for money to go to one of those Negro colleges. Of course, Daddy admired anyone trying to improve their lot in life.

Mother never liked Tommy-Mae. I could never figure out why. Tommy-Mae was the daughter of a Negro woman named Miss Shirley. Miss Shirley used to be the cleaning woman for the company where Mother and Daddy both worked. It was Mother's first job when she returned to town from college. Daddy was already working there. Apparently by the time Mother and Daddy started to date, Miss Shirley had left to start her own laundry cleaning business. I don't know how or why, but Daddy and Miss Shirley remained friends. Daddy had a way with people; all kinds of people. Mother wasn't too happy about having Tommy-Mae as our cleaning girl, but she was happy for the help.

Tommy-Mae did a real good job. Not only did she clean, but she would also cook meals that would last us for a few days. Mother didn't have to rush home to cook. She would come on Tuesdays and Thursdays. On Thursdays, Daddy would take her home. It was a fair exchange, because she and Miss Shirley washed, starched and ironed his work shirts. Miss Shirley had the reputation of doing the best laundry in town. Her services were highly sought after. Everyone said so. She didn't usually do laundry for folks on our block. All of her clients were high-powered businessmen, city officials, and politicians, folks like Mr. Richardson. She charged them a lot more than she charged Daddy. Daddy said it was because of their long-time friendship and him being the one to encourage her to go into business for herself. According to Daddy, if he hadn't been there she wouldn't have done it.

Mother liked the idea that she was using the same service that the rich folks were using, but she didn't really care for Miss Shirley. Mother thought Miss Shirley was sweet on Daddy and Daddy encouraged it. Miss Shirley, and Tommy-Mae, were the subjects of many of their arguments behind closed doors. They thought I couldn't hear them, but I did.

The summer before my senior year, Tommy-Mae, stopped working for us. She had saved enough money to go away to her college. Daddy was so proud of her going to college, that you would have thought it was me going away. He thought smart women were going to rule the world one day. Mother seemed glad she went too. It's funny the details your mind remembers and the forgotten memories your brain retrieves. In order for you to know what made me who I am, you have to hear my thoughts and see these people as I remembered them.

CHAPTER 7

Katherine
(Tea with Mother Richardson)

I had been waiting at the red door for a few minutes, so I decided to ring the bell. Within seconds Miss Josephine, the housekeeper and cook, opened the door. She smelled like fresh string beans.

"Good evening Miss Josephine" I said, in a cheerful tone.

"Why Miss Shelby Baby, come on in" Miss Josephine's warm smile greeted me. "Jonathan is visitin' with his daddy rat now. Let me go git Mrs. Sandra. Let her know yous here."

Miss Josephine smiled all the time. I don't recall one day that I didn't see a smile on her sweet, brown face.

"Miss Sandra, Miss Katherine here!" Miss Josephine yelled over her shoulder.

"Katherine, please join me in my sitting room. Josephine, would you bring Miss Katherine and me some sweet tea." I heard a soft commanding voice coming from down the hall.

"Yes ma'am." Miss Josephine responded.

Miss Josephine headed towards the kitchen and I followed the sound of Mrs. Richardson's voice down a hallway, toward a small office. I had walked past this room any number of times, but had never actually been invited in. I walked into the room and saw her sitting behind a quaint little desk. There was stack of envelopes on one corner. A quick scan of the stack, and I saw what I needed to see. I saw the familiar white envelope sitting on the top of the pile. My heart let out a heavy sigh of relief. I started and couldn't stop smiling. My mood elevated quickly.

"Have a seat, dear." Mrs. Richardson's soft voice filled the space.

My eyes were directed to one of the most beautiful floral chairs I had ever seen in my life. I was almost afraid to sit on it. When I did, it felt like I was sitting on a pile of fluffy feathers. I'm sure I sank a few inches.

Mrs. Sandra Richardson had her head down, concentrating on some correspondence she was in the middle of writing. If you looked at her, you would have seen a woman who couldn't hide her beauty even if she wanted to. She was often dressed in some classic blouse and slim slacks. On this day, she wore a pale blue sweater set with a pair of navy blue straight ankle pants, and a pair of soft leather black slippers. She always reminded me of Mrs. Jackie Kennedy. It was a look she worked to achieve without much effort. She even wore her hair like Mrs. Kennedy. The other women in town also tried to copy that look, even my mother. But Mrs. Richardson had it. Yes, she was a beautiful woman indeed. As I watched her, something about the way she looked, seemed… tired.

"How are you today Katherine dear?" She finally put down her pen and looked at me.

"I'm doing just fine, thank you." I made sure my tone was respectful. "Did Jonathan get to show you the awards and medals he received during assembly today?"

"Yes, dear, he did." She sat back in her chair. "My goodness, you sound as excited about his winning as he is."

"Well Ma'am, I am. I know how important it is to him, that he impress his father." I lowered my voice, "I also know, if you pardon my saying so, just how hard Mr. Richardson is to impress."

Just then, I heard the jingling of glass, behind me. I turned around to see Miss Josephine come into the room carrying a tray. On it was a pitcher of sweet tea and two chilled glasses. The condensation on the glasses led me to believe she must have sat them in the icebox for a few minutes beforehand.

"Thank you, Josephine. Please place the tray, right there,

by the door. That will be all."

There was a small cabinet by the door. Miss Josephine sat the tray down. She winked at me, smiled, and backed out of the room. I smiled and turned back to face Mrs. Richardson. She remained in her seat until Miss Josephine was completely out of the room. She rose and walked over to the cabinet that held the tray. I remained facing forward. I heard her begin to fill each glass. While she poured, she spoke. It was like she was giving, almost, an apology for Mr. Richardson's behavior.

"Edward is indeed a hard man to impress. It's only because he sets high standards for his children. He requires high standards from everyone really."

There was distinct fragrance that arose in the air. I'm sure I smelled rum alcohol for a brief second. It would have been impolite for me to ask or turn around to look. So, I simply received the glass of sweet tea she handed to me. I slowly brought it to my mouth, trying to sniff any signs of rum mixed into the liquid. I smelled nothing. I slowly took a sip. I must have been mistaken. All I could taste was the perfect balance of tea, honey and lemon. While I sipped on my drink, I watched Mrs. Richardson retake her seat behind her desk. She swirled the ice around in her glass before her first sip. After a few minutes and a few more sips, I saw her shoulders relax. She leaned back in her chair. The glass started to feel uncomfortably cold in my hand. I sat it on the ceramic coaster that sat on the small table between the floral chairs.

"Ma'am, my parents and I want to thank the both of you again for arranging for Jonathan and I to have our reception at the Elks Club. I know Mr. Richardson had to pull some strings to make such a thing happen on such short notice." I suddenly felt the need to fill the silence. "Mother was devastated when the Garden banquet hall had to cancel due to the plumbing incident. A wedding reception with no bathrooms would not have been a good thing at all." I took another sip of the delicious tea.

"Nonsense, my dear." She took another long sip from

her glass. "It is our pleasure to do it for you darlings. You know your mother and I have known each other our whole lives? Your mother is actually the reason I met Edward. Your mother knew Edward first, on account of them having had the same math classes." She went on to say with a smile on her face. "She was always a smart cookie, your mother. There she sat in a room filled with men and never did she feel like she didn't have a right to be there. She held her own, she did. You remind me a lot of your mother. You are a smart girl, too. I'm sure people tell you that all the time."

Mrs. Richardson no longer seemed to be talking to me. I could tell she wanted to tell me this story, although mother had told me the same story many times over. I sat back, took another sip of my sweet tea and listened.

"Any way, there she was one of the few girls daring enough to join the advanced math and accounting study groups with the boys. She and Edward were paired up on account of there being an odd number of girls in the group."

She drank the last drop of tea from the bottom of her glass before she continued. "One day, I got out of my history class early and thought I would steal Marian away from her study group, so we could have lunch together. I went to the library to get her and there he was, the most beautiful man I had ever seen. When I walked over to Marian, he stood up, so I knew he was a man raised with manners. He was tall, dark and handsome. Well, one look at Edward and I knew I would be smitten for the rest of my life. We were married soon after and we have been together ever since."

She shook the ice around in her empty glass and looked across her desk smiling at me. I turned my glass up to drink the last of my tea as well. The liquid hitting the back of my parched throat felt like a jump into a cool pool. I was almost embarrassed by how fast I emptied my glass...almost.

"We were such babies then. Not much older than you and Jonathan are now. No matter the age, marriage is a challenge for any young couple… so much pressure. But, you will find that out soon enough."

I sat back in my chair. I was trying to mirror the

relaxing look Mrs. Richardson had taken on after her refreshing glass of sweet tea. She seemed to be lost in her own thoughts as she rambled on about the arrangements for my upcoming nuptials. Looking at her, I could not get away from how breathtakingly beautiful she was. She had natural blond hair that complimented her strong, but delicate, features.

Although Mrs. Richardson found Mr. Richardson strikingly handsome, I always thought his features were awkward and rather distracting. He had all the right ingredients to be handsome. He was tall. I'd say, around, 6'4, or 5, inches tall. His skin was always radiant and looked like he'd been kissed by the sun. He had a strong jawline, dark eyes, and dark hair. His features didn't sit quietly on his face. It was like they couldn't agree on which wanted to stand out the most. Well, I guess it's true what they say about being blinded by love.

The longer I looked at her face, the more I imagined what our future children would look like; Jonathan's and mine. Jonathan's features were dark and heavy like his father's, but they were soft, almost pretty for a guy. It was clear that he inherited that from his mother. I knew our children were going to be beautiful. I watched Mrs. Richardson's mouth move, but I was only partially listening to what she was saying. She said something about guest list and seating arrangements.

I was lost in my own thoughts, about my potential offspring, when the sudden sound of glass breaking startled me out of my haze. My head reflexively turned toward the direction of the sound. It came from the back of the house. I immediately thought of Miss Josephine working in the kitchen. Maybe she dropped a too hot platter. Mother and I did that all the time. I hoped that she was okay. While that thought ran through my mind, I heard the distinctive voice of Mr. Richardson yelling about something. It was an uncomfortable moment. I knew Jonathan was going to speak with his father about our going out of the state to go to college. Maybe they were having a disagreement about that. I felt very fortunate that my parents were happy with whatever my choice would be. Daddy just wanted me to go to college. Mother just wanted me to be with Jonathan. As the yelling continued, I tried to be polite. I turned my attention back to Mrs. Richardson, in front of me, instead of the loud yelling at the back of the house.

"Oh, my dear, looks like you were as parched as I. Would you care for me to refill your glass?" Her voice pierced through my thoughts. Before I could respond, she came around the desk, picked up my glass, and went to the little serving station behind me. She must have quietly closed the door because suddenly the yelling was reduced to an inaudible mumble. From my forward-facing seat I could again hear the slight open and close of the cabinet followed by the sweet, buttery smell of rum. Rum was Daddy's favorite.

That time, for sure, I knew I heard the splash of the liquid being poured into the sweet tea. She handed me my glass before she sat back down. She had refilled her own glass as well. Swirling the ice and brown liquid together in a gentle motion, she leaned back, in the small, cushioned floral chair. Her face softened into a smile.

"Katherine, will I see you and your mother this weekend at the club? We must speak to the chef and get started on planning the dinner menu. One mustn't leave such things till the last minute." She spoke between sips of tea.

"Yes, Mother and I will both be there. Ten o'clock."

Mrs. Richardson looked over the rim of her glass. She replied. "I do hope Marian is not offended by my involvement in so many of the details of this ceremony. My only daughter robbed me of the opportunity to plan her wedding by running off with that boy from college. I must say, you have been so sweet to allow me to take part."

"No ma'am, not at all. Actually, I believe she is a little relieved." I reassured her. "Mother is not very good at showy events. Do you remember my sweet sixteen party she tried to plan? I almost died of embarrass..."

The sentence was barely out of my mouth, before Jonathan came bursting into the room. He scooped me out of my chair and gave me a hug so tight my ribs hurt.

"Jonathan Wallace Richardson! Is this the way we enter a closed room? Son, where are your manners?" Mrs. Richardson stood up from her chair to chastise her son.

"I apologize mother. I just found out that Katie was here. All my senses fly right out of my head when I know she's around."

The words poured out of Jonathan's mouth. He had a smile on his face so bright, I'm sure it shamed the sun. He looked at me like I was the last biscuit left on the serving plate and he was eager to get to it before anyone else could. His eyes never left my face the whole time he spoke to his mother. I could've been embarrassed by it, but I wasn't. I loved his attention.

"Josephine wanted to know if Katie was staying for dinner so she can set a place for her at the table." He was still staring at me with that smile.

"Yes, that sounds like an excellent idea. Katherine dear, please say you'll join us." Mrs. Richardson had wiggled her way in between her son and me, so that she was the one staring me in the face.

"Thank you, Mrs. Richardson. I should first..."

She tilted my face and grabbed both my shoulders, so that I was forced to match her eye contact. Her face was uncharacteristically stern.

"Dear, we are going to be family. You should stop calling me Mrs. Richardson. Why, you'll be a 'Mrs. Richardson', yourself, soon enough. I insist you call me mother!"

The flash of her mood change caught me completely off guard.

I said. "Thank you Mrs...I mean Mother Richardson, but I should check home with my parents first."

"Aren't you such the good daughter? Well, run along and hurry back. We still have much to talk about, concerning this wedding." And just like that, her face softened back to its former self.

"Mother, I can take Katie home right quick." Jonathan

said looking down at me from behind his mother.

Mrs. Richardson responded to Jonathan. "Sweetheart, now that I think about it, we can simply place a phone call to find out."

Mother Richardson continued holding my shoulders. She had me at arm's length and didn't let me go. She turned her head to look over her shoulder at Jonathan's face. I locked eyes with him, over the petite woman's head. My cheeks warmed up and I could feel myself begin to blush.

He replied. "Yes mother, that is true, but Katie and I wanted to go for a drive before dinner."

She looked back at me and smiled. She released her grip on my shoulders and went back to her seat behind her desk. I stood next to Jonathan and turned to face her. Mother Richardson picked up her glass, swirled the ice around in the sweet tea, and took a long sip. She gave me a knowing smile.

"Of course, you two darlings want some alone time. Trust me, I know what it's like to be young and in love." Jonathan reached over and took my hand. My hand looked tiny and lost in his. Mother Richardson took another sip and continued." You want to spend every waking minute together. You want to share every experience with each other." She paused and that stern look returned to her face. "Jonathan, I do expect you to be a perfect gentleman with our dear Katherine. She is a good girl and we want to keep it that way... at least until the wedding." She put her free hand over her mouth and let out a soft giggle.

"Don't worry mother, I'm always a gentleman with Katie." He turned up the wattage on his smile.

"Ok, darling Katherine, I hope I'll see you at dinner later. Do say hello to both your parents for me."

"Yes Mrs. -I mean Mother Richardson. I will." As I grabbed my sweater, I motioned to Jonathan to come closer. I whispered in his ear to grab the large white envelope from the stack on top of his mother's desk. As he reached past me to pick it up, I noticed some blood near his ear on the back of his head.

"My goodness Jonathan, you're bleeding!"

My voice came out louder than I expected. Startled, Jonathan slapped his hand over the cut. He and his mother locked eyes, exchanged a quick glance, and looked away. The brief moment felt like not being let in on some secret that only they knew.

"It's nothing serious. Let's go." Jonathan said as he tugged on my hand and led me out of the room.

"Jonathan maybe you should have that looked at." I told him with concern.

"Katie, you're making way too much out of this. Guys get bruises all the time. It's life. Hold on."

I waited in the hall, while Jonathan went back into the office, to kiss his mother goodbye. Instead of going out the front door, which was closer, we headed toward the kitchen. Before we were out of hearing range, Mother Richardson called to us, "Please be on time for dinner. You know how your father feels about starting dinner on time!"

Miss Josephine was in the kitchen, stirring something in a large pot on the stove. It smelled divine. Jonathan told her to set a place-setting at the table for me. I wanted to sneak a peek into her big pot. I said. "Miss Josephine, I don't know what you're cookin, but it sure does smell good." I thought I saw her mouth move in response, but Jonathan was in too much of a hurry for me to hear whatever she said. He tugged on my hand and pulled me along, quickly. We exited the house, through the garden doors off the kitchen. Mr. Pete was still working. He had moved on to the projects in the backyard.

"My keys, Pete?" Jonathan yelled over his shoulder, while we headed towards his car.

"I puts them on the front seat Mr. Jonathan, same as always." Mr. Pete yelled back in a calm tone.

Before I get into the car, I made eye contact with Mr. Pete.

I gave a short wave and said, "You have a fine evening Mr. Pete."

"You do the same Miss Shelby."

That time, he stopped working long enough to look me directly in the eyes. Those brief seconds of eye contact revealed something behind his eyes. He returned his attention back to his task. I wasn't sure what I saw, but I knew saw something.

CHAPTER 8

Katherine
(At the Water Tower)

Jonathan and I sat quietly. We held hands, while he drove down the open road. It was the road that led out of town. We were both glad to finally be alone for the first time that long day. He let go of my hand so that he could fidget with the radio. I knew he wanted to talk about the track meet, and what his coach said later in the locker room, but my mind wondered back to what happened, moments before we got here.

We had gone home to ask Mother for permission to have dinner at the Richardson's. I also wanted to pick up my letter to show Jonathan. Mother wasn't home yet. Daddy said she had gotten hung up in some city board meeting and wouldn't be home for a while. I asked Daddy for permission and he said that it would be fine, long as I came home right after.

"She may be your future bride, but she will always be my daughter!" Daddy looked Jonathan straight in the eyes while he spoke, to let him know he meant business.

"I'll be sure to bring her straight home, Sir!" Jonathan said in his best Clark Kent impression. Daddy looked past Jonathan, to me. He gave me the nod, okay.

"Great, thank you!" I said to Jonathan, "I just need to grab something out of my room, then we can go". I looked back at my father. "Daddy, please be nice to him."

"Of course, Chipmunk. . . ain't I always nice?"

It wasn't that Daddy disliked like Jonathan, it was just that he was suspicious of his boy-next-door charm. Also, Daddy, unlike Mother, thought I could do better. He felt

Jonathan was nowhere near my intellectual match.

"Somethin' ain't right in that house!" Daddy would rant to Mother and me over and over again. Mother always dismissed him, by saying a father would never find any man good enough for his daughter. She'd say that Daddy 'would find something wrong with a three-legged table no matter how well put together or how sturdy'. Whenever he started to drone on about it, she would fuss and tell Daddy to hush up.

"Leave that girl alone Tom. Can't you see she loves that boy?" Mother would say.

Daddy could never tell us what he specifically thought 'wasn't right' in the Richardson's house. It was just that something didn't settle right with him. Mother and I would roll our eyes and ignore him whenever he got on his soapbox about the righteous behaviors of a man. He would say it was just a feeling passed down to him through his family line. His daddy had it and his daddy before him. He didn't talk much about his family. He lost my grandmother when he was just a baby and my grandfather never remarried, so, when he died, Daddy lost the only family he knew. Mother and I were all that he had.

I grabbed the acceptance letter out of the hatbox in my closet and ran back to the front room. As I stumbled in, I was surprised to find my two men were actually having a conversation. They didn't notice me, at first. Being on the tailend of the discussion, I didn't quite know what that they were conversing about. I stood there and watched them for a brief moment, before I said, "Okay, I'm ready!"

Jonathan looked at me.

He spoke to my father. "I'll have her home right after dinner Mr. Shelby".

Jonathan let out a small sigh and it looked like his shoulders relaxed. He was relieved that I was back.

Daddy asked. "That should be no later than eight thirty then, right young man?" He looked Jonathan straight in his eyes, to show he was serious.

Daddy often said, *"If a man can't look you in the eyes when he's talkin' to you, he either up to sumpthin or he's lyin'! And you don't want no part of either one."* It was his motto, of sorts. They were words he lived by, and I suspect, it was probably due to all them years as a salesman. Thank goodness, Jonathan returned Daddy's eye contact.

"Yes Sir!" They shook hands, and Jonathan thanked him. We walked back to the car holding hands with a big smile on our faces and Daddy peeking out of the window. It's so funny how my brain works. Each memory reminds me of another memory. Everything leads back to everything else. Life's funny that way.

Anyway, I was thinking about that moment, when my mind was jolted back to the car ride. My thoughts were interrupted by Jonathan's failed attempt at singing along to the Beach Boy tune, "California Girl." It was so loud and bad all I could do was laugh and plead with him to stop. We kept driving and tried our best to sing whatever song came on the radio.

Whenever we really wanted to be alone, we drove out to the water tower. It was only about 20 miles on the outside of town, but it felt like miles away from everything we knew. The tower sat in an open field of grass and wildflowers. As we drove there, that day, I read my acceptance letter aloud. I was offered a full academic scholarship, which included housing. After I finished reading, I looked over at him. He gave me that sunshine look of his and I thought I would melt, right there in the seat of his car. I loved that smile, like nature made special for me. We decided until we were at the tower to read his letter.

Jonathan parked the car on the side of the road out of the way of traffic. We grabbed the blanket we kept in his trunk and walked over to the tower. By that point, we were both too nervous and excited to sit. So, we stood under the tower, leaning on the cement blocks that held the steel beams of the tower in place.

"I'm so proud of you Katie! I always knew you were a smart one." Jonathan was beaming.

"Thank you, sweetie, now stop stalling and read yours before I burst!"

Although I knew what the letter would say, I wanted to hear him read the words with my own ears.

"You know I'm not good at reading out loud! You read it for me." Jonathan handed me the letter.

I reached for the paper and leaned back across from him.

"You don't have to read the whole thing. Just the part where I get in and I get a scholarship too!" His voice was excited as mine.

I knew the format of acceptance letters pretty well, at that point, so, I knew exactly where to look. I read him the "We would like to offer you" and the "Financial Aid offer" portion of the letter. Jonathan was accepted with a full athletic scholarship which also included housing. When he heard that, he let out a big "Yahoo!!!" His smile was so bright and wide, it could have scorched the grass around us. He was so proud of himself. I was proud of him, too. He lifted me up and spun around. He squeezed me so tight I thought my ribs would break. He put me down and walked around the beam.

"Katie, you know what this means. We get to live together on campus. We get to start our lives together as a married couple, free from this small town and its small-town dreams. We get to dream big!"

We both plopped down on the blanket beneath the tower and looked up at the Georgia sun. It was nearly 4:30, and the sun felt as hot as it felt at noon. We laughed and we talked. We talked over each other in our excitement about our lives on campus. We tried to imagine how life would be different, living up north in a strange new town. What kinda friends would we make? We both agreed we needed to start watching the evening news more, so we could practice how to sound more northern like. I thought it would be a good idea to live on campus for the first year only, so we could get a feeling of college life and the city life. Our sophomore year, we could look for an off-campus apartment. Both my parents had lived in the dorms their whole time in college. They told me stories of wild parties and indecent mishaps that took place in their dorm rooms. With what I knew about my

Jonathan, we needed to be as far away from distractions as we could get.

I continued lying on my back and telling him my thoughts and plans for us. I turned my head to look at him. His expression had changed and a seriousness replaced his smile. I kept on talking about what I thought I knew about college life. Jonathan stopped adding to the conversation.

I finally came right out and asked him. "Baby, why you get so quiet?"

"Well you are making all these moves already and we haven't even gotten there yet." He said in a solemn tone.

"I'm just talkin' Jonathan. I have no more idea how this is all gonna turn out than you do. I just know how important it's gonna be for us to stay focused in order for us both to get through college. From what Mother and Daddy say, we will be doing ourselves a big favor by putting some space between us and all the foolishness." I thought my matter of fact thinking made sense.

"But if we move off campus, won't we lose our scholarships?" He asked.

"No, we won't lose our scholarships, but we will only get a stipend toward our apartment rent. It won't be fully covered like if we were staying in the dorms. We would have to find a way to cover the rest ourselves."

I watched Jonathan's face. He continued looking up at the sky.

"How would we be able to cover the rest? I won't be able to work with all the practice I'll be doing. Between classes and sports, when would I have time for a job?"

"Well Jonathan, I just thought with some help from your parents and my parents we should be ok."

"We ain't askin' our folks for nothing once we get outta here! You hear me?" I watched as a dark grey shadow fell over Jonathan's face. I looked up at the sky to see if there was a cloud that had flown over him. I didn't see any clouds. The sky was bright and clear. I looked back at Johnathan. I could tell he was getting concerned how we would be able to manage all of it.

I tried to reassure him. "I don't think we'll be asking for a lot. Why, the most expensive part is the tuition, and we both have that covered. We would only need a little help with rent and maybe food. Daddy says-"

Before I could finish my sentence, Jonathan turned towards me and interrupted.

He shouted in my face. "We ask nothing from our folks! I'm going to be your husband by then. I'm the one who will be responsible for taking care of us. Not your daddy. Not my father. Me!" His voice was so intense, it startled me. With his face so close to mine, I saw a mixture of hurt, confusion, and anger.

It dawned on me that my Jonathan never worked a day in his young, rich life. He had never had to balance a budget or be careful about how he spent money. I, however, had gotten a job every summer, since I was 14, back when I babysat for the Johnsons, across the street. There was a summer where I worked at the Five and Dime lunch counter. Last summer I worked at Daddy's company, filing papers. I had always had a savings account as far back as I could remember.

Mother and Daddy always made me aware of our money situation. They explained, it was so that I knew why some things I'd had to wait for, if I wanted them. I honestly lived a very charmed life, I'm sure. Being the only child to Marian and Thomas Shelby, I never had to suffer for anything. But, as I told you, we did have some lean years. There were times where we had to watch our pennies to get by. Mother passed on to me the importance of money management. Daddy passed on to me the necessity of saving for the important stuff and putting away something for a rainy day. So, we weren't Richardson money, but we were doing better than a whole lot of others. My parents were both geniuses when it came to money management.

"Jonathan, why would we make college harder on ourselves than we need to? My parents have been saving my whole life to be able to do two things. One of them was for my wedding, and with the assistance of your Mother, that cost has been cut in half. The other was my college education. I have a full academic scholarship. Daddy feels that the money he saved for my schooling should still be used to help me get through college. That could mean books, rent, food, whatever I need to get through and finish. I'm sure Daddy would..."

Jonathan abruptly rolled on top of me. His face hovered above mine. We were so close our noses were touching. That dark cloud had overshadowed his face. There was nothing but coldness behind his eyes. Gone was any of that sunshine that brightened my day just a few minutes before. I didn't know it at the time, but, in its place was a smoldering tornado that threatened to tear up everything in its path.

Jonathan yelled at me. "I thought I said we were doing this without our folks help! Maybe, you're not so smart, if you can't understand that no help means no kind of help! No money for rent, no money for food or books or anything."

I could feel the heat of his breath in my face. Jonathan had his full weight on top of me. In addition to being in shock, I was also struggling for air.

"Jonathan, I can't breathe, you're hurting me!" I pleaded.

He rolled over and sat up. I sat up immediately and held my hand over my heart. I waited for the pressure pain to subside. My body ached from his weight. His reaction was confusing.

I spoke in a soft voice. "Baby, I don't understand. We've talked about this before. Why are you now so upset about our parents helping us with some of the simple?"

He grabbed both of my arms and pulled me in close to him. His face was jammed so close to mind, I thought he was going to bite my nose off, when he began to speak.

"Katherine, why are you trying to make me angry? I'm telling you how this is going to work. Don't you believe I know what I'm doing? Don't you believe in me? Don't you believe I can take care of you as your husband? If you don't believe in me, then why are we even getting married?" He was shouting. I didn't move. I was afraid to move. We just looked at each other for what felt like minutes, but I'm sure were only seconds. I watched the storm on his face turn into cloudy confusion. Pain and hurt replaced the anger. He let me go. He stood up and walked a few feet away, leaving me to sit back on my hands in the tall soft grass. The many questions banging around in my head got stuck in my throat. Fear kept them from spilling out. Not knowing how my voice would be received, kept me silent. I had never experienced this Jonathan before. I didn't know how to proceed forward. What words to say?

I remained silent as I watched him continue to walk toward his car and away from me. Ten minutes must have passed as we both stayed in our own worlds inside our heads. I saw him look at his watch, then back at me. He started walking back in my direction. As he got closer to me, I didn't lift my head. He loomed over me just standing there. Not knowing what to expect, I didn't dare make eye contact. I looked past his legs into the distance. After a brief pause, he extended his hands to me. I looked up at his face. I looked into those eyes. The storm had passed. Gone were the grey clouds. What remained was a humbled look of hurt and embarrassment.

"Come on Katie, I told my mother that we would be on time for dinner. We need'a leave now." His tone was soft.

Without saying a word, I allowed his outstretched hands to pull me to my feet. We walked back to his car, in silence. We drove, in silence, the whole way back into town and back to his house. Neither one of us said much during dinner either. Mr. Richardson asked how my parents were doing. Mrs. Richardson had an on-going conversation by herself. She went on and on about the guest list, which city officials should get an invitation, the color scheme and the table centerpieces. I don't think she noticed at all that I hadn't spoken. The only time she stopped talking was when she refilled her glass of sweet tea.

CHAPTER 9

Jonathan
(At the Water Tower)

Jonathan had been looking forward to being alone with Katie since the afternoon track meet. After the horrible encounter with his father, her company was just the comfort he needed. Katie was always in a good mood. Her good mood made his mood good every time. Seeing her in his mother's office was perfect timing. It was a short drive over to Katie's house. They were going to ask permission from her parents, to join his family for dinner. Jonathan was looking forward to the day when permission would not be needed. They would be married as husband and wife and they wouldn't need to ask anyone's permission, for anything.

Katie's mother was absent. When they pulled up to the front of her house, her mother's car was not there, but her father was home. Mr. Shelby made Jonathan nervous. He had wanted to wait in the car. It would only take Katie a moment to run in and ask. Katie wouldn't go for it, though.

"How you think my daddy's gonna feel about my fiancé, not walking me to the door? You want his permission, you gonna have to ask for it, like a man."

Jonathan got out of the car and followed Katie into the house. When they entered the living room, Mr. Shelby moved his newspaper from his lap, and stood up. He extended his hand. Jonathan took it and gave it a firm shake.

"Good evening Mr. Shelby."

Jonathan could tell Mr. Shelby didn't really like him. He never understood why, just that he wasn't liked. Mrs. Shelby loved him. He kind of wished she was there at that moment. Katie went to her room to get her letter from the University of Illinois, she had received that day. Jonathan hoped she got accepted. This was their last shot at getting into the same college together. It wouldn't be the same experience if she wasn't by his side. Katie was a smart girl. She shouldn't have had any problems getting into the school. He thought to himself. Besides, she filled out her application the same way she did his, so that should count for something.

He thought about sitting down and then thought better of it. He watched Mr. Shelby pour himself a drink of rum and cola and sat back down in his recliner. He looked up at Jonathan, above the rim of his glasses, and motioned him to take a seat. Jonathan obliged. He sat across from the recliner on a plain, brown ottoman.

"So, young man, have you decided what school you want to attend yet?"

Jonathan didn't want to appear indecisive, so he said the only college he could think of.

"Yes Sir. I'm thinking it will most likely be the University of Illinois in Chicago, Sir." He tried to sound casual and confident.

Mr. Shelby replied. "They have an excellent athletic program there. That would be an excellent choice for you. And I'm sure you know my Katherine wants to become a journalist. Illinois would be a good choice for both of you."

"Yes, Sir it would." Jonathan had no clue if the college offered Journalism or not. He was just glad that it appeared to have pleased Mr. Shelby.

"You know son, you will be marrying my daughter soon... in a few weeks to be exact." Mr. Shelby was looked directly into Jonathan's eyes. "Part of being a husband is being able to provide for both yourself and your wife. It will be up to you to make sure she has all that she needs. Do you think you are responsible enough to take on that task, son?" Jonathan took a deep breath as his earlier situation with his father replayed over in his head. A small knot formed in the pit of his stomach. He was determined not to let Mr. Shelby see him crumble the way his father had.

"No need to worry, Sir, I will be more than capable of

providing for Katie and me." He tried to mimic the pitch and tone of Mr. Shelby's voice, in his own.

"I know our little family doesn't have the type of wealth your family is used to, but my daughter has not had to want for anything." Mr. Shelby swirled the ice in his glass around before bringing the cup to his lips. "I just need your assurance that she will continue to have her needs met."

The vision of Mr. Shelby's glass and the smell of the alcohol made Jonathan's stomach tighten.

Mr. Shelby continued. "I don't like the idea of you two getting married so soon out of high school. I think you should wait until you both finish you schoolin', that way I can continue taking care of her while she's doin' her studies. But... you kids are hell bent on getting hitched now. I don't see why it's so urgent. I do know, that once she becomes your wife, that becomes your job. Are you sure you can handle all of that and school?" Mr. Shelby stood up and continued to look at Jonathan waiting for an answer. He walked toward a long cabinet that held several crystal decanters. He took the top off of one and poured the brown liquid into his short clear glass. Jonathan stood up.

"You have my promise, sir. I will make sure Katie has everything she needs." He said.

Katie entered the room. Both men turned in her direction. Mr. Shelby spoke a few more words about a man's responsibility and the job he takes on when he marries. Jonathan nodded in agreement and listened, politely.

During a natural pause in the conversation, Katie interjected. "Okay, I'm ready." She gave her father a kiss on the cheek.

"Have a good time, chipmunk." He kissed his daughter back.

Jonathan reassured Mr. Shelby. "Don't worry sir. I'll have her home right after dinner." He was relieved Katie had come when she did.

"That means she should be home no later than eight thirty then, right young man?"

Mr. Shelby stood around 6 feet even, so he had to look

up to Jonathan's 6'3". Jonathan still felt small in his presence. His stature was not as frightening as his father's, but Jonathan always had the feeling that he would never be able to measure up to the man that raised the girl of his dreams. But he was going to try.

Jonathan shook Mr. Shelby's hand while looking him directly in the eyes. "Yes, Sir."

Katie read Jonathan her acceptance letter, on the ride over to their favorite spot. It was just outside of town. It was an old water tower. He always loved the open space and the endless scenery of wild flowers and tall grass. According to the letter, Katie was gonna receive a full scholarship. That meant everything would be paid for and they wouldn't need her father for anything. Jonathan couldn't stop smiling at the thought of her father thinking Jonathan was the one taking care of everything. He would have to tell Katie not to tell her father about the money.

Jonathan was in a good mood. They parked the car just off the road and grabbed the blanket he kept in his trunk just for such occasions. Katie didn't like to sit directly on the grass. They laid the blanket under the tower, but they were too excited to sit down. Jonathan had sent out several applications, with Katie's help. All of them came back; "Sorry, we are unable to admit you at this time." This was really his last chance to get into an out of state college before he had to register for the local two-year college. Jonathan really didn't want to have to do that, like some of his classmates from high school. He just needed to prove to his old man that he was better than that. He needed to prove he had what it took, to make it without his father's money. He needed to prove that his sports talent could indeed get him what he wanted for his life. Jonathan also knew that as long as he was in his small town, he would forever be compared to his super smart, superman of a father, Edward Richardson. It was always going to be a competition between him and his father and that was a race he knew he would lose. Jonathan knew his father didn't compete fairly. His father found ways to beat his competitor, before the race even began.

Katie was the only one who understood how much he needed to get away from his father, but even she didn't know the whole story. He left out many of the embarrassing details of his encounters with his king-like father. He never told her how many times his father had degraded him or minimized him. He never told her how often he still had trouble controlling his bladder, when his father yelled at him. Never told about the ridicule he would receive after he peed himself. How many times he had raced home to show his father some accomplishment from an athletic event, a trophy or medal, only to have it destroyed and/or belittled. Jonathan knew he wouldn't be a man in his Katie's eyes if she knew how many times he cried after time spent with his father. All she did know was that his father was hard to please and Jonathan was tired of trying to please him. He wanted out and this letter was his last chance.

Jonathan paced in circles, while trying to open the thick envelope. He ripped it open, but he was too nervous to read it. He handed the whole package over to Katie. She was always able to get to the meat of the letters quickly. Besides, when he was that nervous, some of the big words would take him too long to figure out. That would make him even more nervous. Katie started to read the letter out loud. The more she read, the bigger his smile got. Jonathan couldn't believe his luck. He was accepted. Not only that, but he was being offered a full athletic scholarship. Coach was right. His athletic skills had paid off. He couldn't wait to tell his father that bit of news.

Jonathan and Katie lied on their backs under the tower. They looked up at the sky and made plans for their future. As Katie rambled on about making friends and the difference in northern weather, Jonathan released a heavy sigh of relief. It unburdened him from the heavy conversations he had earlier with his father and Katie's father. Now all they had to do was go to school. He didn't have to feel like a failed husband before he even started.

Just as he was finding peace, knowing that the money issue was solved, Katie started to talk about asking her father for money. It was so that they could get an apartment.

They went back and forth about the necessity of moving off campus and taking on that additional cost. Jonathan tried to convince Katie that living on campus with housing covered was the best way to go. He didn't want to tell her about the talk he had with her father, and the concerns about Jonathan's ability to provide for her. He didn't want her to agree with her father when he said they should wait until they finished college before getting married.

Jonathan started to feel the knot in his stomach tighten. He was beginning to feel rejected by his soon-to-be bride. Why was she insisting on doing it the hard way? Why would she even bring the money issue up when they already had it resolved? The more Katie talked, the more Jonathan felt insulted and hurt. She of all people was supposed to have faith in him. He didn't know how to stop the back and forth. He recalled situations he witnessed between his parents. Mother would make a suggestion, Father would make the decision. That was that. There was no back and forth. After listening to Katie go on for a while, Jonathan put his foot down.

"We ain't askin' our folks for nothing once we get outta here!" He said, with the best imitation of his father he could manage.

But the conversation was not resolved. Katie still had more questions and suggestions about the decision he had made. He felt that familiar tingle in his bladder. He got the urge to go to the bathroom whenever he felt anxious. Why was there still conversation about this? His mother never questioned his father. How dare she even suggest they needed their parents help?

The longer Katie talked, the more upset he became. He had to let her know that he was the husband here. As the husband, he would be providing for whatever they needed. There would be no running back to daddy. But, Katie kept on talking. Through all of the many things Katie said, all Jonathan could hear was how unreliable he was. Her father had always taken care of what she needed, and she expected him to do it during her years in college. He listened as long as he could. The conversation he had with himself told him he had to put an end to it. He had to get her attention and make her listen.

Jonathan rolled over on top of Katie, and pushed his face into her, until they were nose to nose. Katie got quiet. Satisfied that he got her to listen, he made sure she knew that he was going to be her husband. He was going to be the one who would be responsible for their well-being.

He heard himself shout. "Not your father. Not my father. Me!"

It worked. She was listening. Jonathan wanted Katie to understand that she didn't need to rely on anyone but him. She just needed to see the wisdom in his words. He wanted her to see that she needed to stop thinking she was smarter than he was, and just let him be the one in charge of their plans. At that point, Jonathan had her pinned down and he began to feel her struggle beneath him. He realized he might have been hurting her with his weight. She complained that she needed air. Since she had quieted down, he let her go and sat up next to her on the blanket. He wanted to explain why he made that hard choice. Katie didn't give him time to think. She just started back into questioning him... questioning his mindset... questioning his ability to handle things.

Jonathan grew angry. *"What is wrong with this girl?"* He thought to himself. *"Is she just trying to test me? What would it take for her to get it?"* After a while the voice he heard was no longer Katie's voice. It was his father's voice. It was his father's doubting, smug judgment of Jonathan's intelligence, laughing at him. He was beyond upset. He needed the noise to stop. He got right in her face again. He had some questions of his own. Why didn't she trust him? Why did she doubt him? She needed to just let him do this.

The voice in his head took a pause, when Jonathan looked at the love of his life. She was still talking. All he wanted was to silence her into submission. When he spoke to her, he looked her directly in her eyes. He heard the voice again.

"A real man always looks you in the eye when he talks to

you."

Jonathan thought that's what Mr. Shelby would have done. He grabbed her on both sides of her shoulders. "I'm telling you how this is going to be!" He said firmly. Her abrupt silence gave him a surge of power. It made him feel like he was in charge. Jonathan stared into Katie's eyes. He had hoped to see respect for his taking control, but all he saw was fear. Her fear startled him. It was not what he had expected. He let her go, got up, and walked away. He never wanted to be the cause of that fear in anybody. He knew that fear.

He was unsure of how to take his actions back, so he put some space between Katie and himself, by standing alone. They remained silent for a while until Jonathan realized they needed to start heading back, if they were going to be on time for dinner. He walked over to her and put out his hands to help her up on her feet. She looked up from the blanket and allowed him to pull her up. He let out a soft sigh. Jonathan and Katie rode to his house wrapped in the quiet of their own thoughts. Jonathan knew he had behaved in a way that Katie may not forgive. She was not used to dealing with any other man but her father. He thought to himself, *"We are going to be husband and wife real soon. She needs to start getting used to me taking on more of the head of household role."*

The voice in his head agreed and told him he had done the right thing. *"The sooner she can get used to you being in charge, the happier y'all will both be."*

Although he thought this, Jonathan sat in silence across the table from Katie during dinner. He had time to replay the look of fear on her face. Maybe he was a bit more aggressive than he had meant to be. After all Katie was a delicate woman, like his mother. After dinner, he would apologize to her on the ride back to her house.

CHAPTER 10

Katherine
(I'm Sorry)

I sat in the passenger seat, next to Jonathan, as he drove me home. I was in a better mood. I'm sure the excellent dinner Miss Josephine prepared for us that evening had something to do with it. She had served smothered chicken, homemade buttermilk biscuits, string beans, and garlic and butter mashed potatoes… and of course, sweet tea. Everything was delicious. During dinner, Mother Richardson's continued conversation about the wedding did not require my input at all. This gave me plenty of time to think over the events that had unfolded earlier at the water tower.

I had never experienced Jonathan like that before. I knew he had a temper. I had seen him lose it with some of his team mates, but he had never directed it towards me. One time, after a basketball game, his best friend Matt was teasing him about a layup or free throw shot, whatever it's called. Jonathan missed the shot and Matt ended up making the winning basket. Matt was feeling proud of himself at Jonathan's expense. He started letting Jonathan have it with the jokes and teasing. It was a rare moment when Jonathan's father was in attendance at the game. I wasn't there. It all happened in the locker room. But the guys say it took four guys to get Jonathan off of poor Matt. Of course, the next day, they were back to being best friends. Jonathan told me about it himself that night on the phone. He blamed it on the stress of trying to perform in front of his father. He claimed it was just too much pressure on him and to have Matt tease him was just more than he could take. Matt understood and forgave him. Certainly, if Matt forgave him, then so could I.

I was sure he was feeling that same kind of pressure after his meet and earlier that day. I should have known. He had also had a conversation with his father right after that. His father always caused him stress. He hadn't told me very much about what was said just that it didn't go as smoothly as he would have liked. Then I started in on him with all my endless questions. I'm sure the pressure just caught up to him. Yes, that was how I rationalized it in my head. Maybe Mother was right. I did need to learn when to be quiet and when to just listen.

When I looked at him, across the dinner table, he looked relaxed, like my old Jonathan. That was the confirmation I needed. His behavior at the water tower had to have just been the stress taking its toll on him. Me, and all my questions, just added to it. I had to apologize. Since I was able to understand the reasoning behind his behavior, I also began to relax. I enjoyed the rest of dinner time with the Richardsons.

So, there we were in his car. We rode for at least five minutes in silence. I couldn't imagine what he thought of me. I should have been his support, instead I added to his turbulent day. I needed to make this right. I tried to figure out the proper words I wanted to say.

Another minute went by, and then we both blurted out, in unison, "I'M SORRY!"

The harmonizing blend of our voices in the car startled both of us. We just looked at each other for a second. I started to laugh, then he laughed, and then we were both laughing. We laughed so hard I thought we were gonna pee our pants, right there in the car.

"Katie, I'm so sorry! You know the last thing in this world I ever want to do is hurt you." Jonathan pulled the car over about a block from my house.

"I know that Jonathan, I'm sorry too. I should have never questioned you like that." We both stroked each other's cheeks, wiping away the tears that started to cascade down.

"When you kept on asking questions like that, it made me think you didn't trust me." He said softly.

I nodded. "I know, and I'm sorry. Of course, I trust you."

I put my fingers to his lips. He kissed them and held on to my hand the rest of the short drive. We got to my house with ten minutes to spare, before I had to be in for the night. We sat in the car and talked about our soon-to-be future. That time, we didn't argue, we just talked. Everything was happening so fast it was head-spinning. As the conversation progressed, I told him about the incident with Peggy at the track meet. We both laughed. It felt good to be back to normal. The whole time we were in the car, we saw Daddy peeking through the living room drapes. Finally, he just turned the porch light on. We knew that was our cue. Jonathan walked me to the door. We had just stepped onto the first step when Daddy opened the door.

"Well, thank you for getting my baby girl home at a respectable time and all in one piece. I thought I was going to have to rescue her from your car for a moment there." Daddy shook Jonathan's hand, and then gave me a big hug and kiss.

"Oh Daddy, stop!" I said, embarrassed by Daddy's over-the-top display of affection.

"Of course, sir... but you know, in a few weeks, she will be *my* baby girl!" The reaction on Daddy's face made Jonathan chuckle uncomfortably. I think Jonathan thought he was being funny. I also knew that Daddy didn't find it funny at all. He looked Jonathan directly in his eyes, with a very stern expression. It looked funny to me due to their difference in height and Daddy having to look up to Jonathan. It was just funny, that's all.

"Let me make myself very clear young man, Katherine Frances Shelby will always be *my* baby girl!" Daddy declared.

Jonathan's eyes got wide and his smirk disappeared.

"Oh... of course sir... I mean yes, Sir. I didn't mean to imply-"

Daddy didn't let him finish. "Good night Son. Say good night to Katherine."

I walked up the steps and into the house. Daddy started to close the door.

"Good night Jonathan." I yelled over Daddy's shoulder.

"Good night baby, I mean Katherine. Good night sir."

Jonathan said his last good nights to a closed door.

CHAPTER 11

Katherine
(The Wedding Night)

The next few days of school flew by in a blur. Between finals and graduation practice, it had become clear that those were the last days of our group being together. Many of us had been in the same schools since kindergarten. To add salt to the wound, we were the 1st class to have so many of our students going out of state to college. Everyone made promises of getting together for holidays and staying in touch. We all knew somehow that wouldn't happen. But we made the promises anyway.

My best friend at the time was Jennifer Wilcox. She and I were one of the ones who had known each other since kindergarten. We shared the same nap mat. A lot of bonding can happen when you take naps together. We were best friends from then on. Like me, she was going out of state for college. She was headed to California, to some school called The University of Southern California. It was in Los Angeles. That was a long way from The University of Illinois, at Chicago. We promised to meet up over the Christmas break or spring break. That turned out to be a promise that never happened, but at the time we swore we would.

The day of graduation was bittersweet. We turned the auditorium into a nightclub and served sparkling apple cider in champagne glasses. We were adults now. We partied and laughed so hard, I can't remember when we all had so much fun. None of the boys ended the evening in a fight which was how our class normally ended a school dance. That night we held each other tight. It was magical.

Then came the day of the wedding. Jonathan's father

being who he was, made it kind of a big deal in our tiny town. All the local papers were there taking pictures. I must say we were all so grown up looking that day. We had five bridesmaids and five groomsmen. Matt was Jonathan's best man and of course Jennifer was my maid of honor. My colors were pink and grey. The bridesmaids all wore soft pink chiffon gowns. The groomsmen wore grey tuxedos. My Jonathan wore a black tuxedo with a grey vest to match the groomsmen. I wore a gown made of chiffon and silk. The bodice was sprinkled with hand sewn pink pearls all over it. It flowed away from my body in layers of soft white silk and pale shades of pink chiffon that matched my bridesmaids. Mother was against my adding in the pale pink. She thought it would cause the town to talk. People would say that I was some kind of loose girl who couldn't wear white. I felt like a princess.

Mother 's dress was similar to the bridesmaids but in a deep fuchsia pink, my favorite color. She was stunning. Daddy almost choked on his gum when he saw her. Daddy cried the whole time he walked me down the aisle. Once we got to the altar, just before he placed my hand in Jonathans, he hugged me really tight. He looked at me with the most loving look I had ever received from him and told me softly through tears, "You will always be my baby girl!"

"I know Daddy." I whispered back and kissed him on his tear drenched cheek.

The Richardsons hosted the reception at the Elks Club. It was a very private country club where you had to be invited to join. For some of us, it would be our first and probably our last time ever seeing the inside of that place. We were in a large ballroom. Mother Richardson did a wonderful job with the decorations. Every table was draped in white linen and had a centerpiece of soft pink roses in beautiful crystal vases. Each vase had the name of one of the members of the wedding party engraved on it. There was a live band and an open bar. The bar was supposed to require I. D. before serving alcohol to anyone who didn't look of age, but most of the guests were from our senior class. I don't recall anyone under the age of eighteen attending. All of our friends took complete advantage of the bar.

By the end of the night everyone was pretty much snookered. My parents were actually having a good time. I can't recall ever hearing my mother laugh out loud the way she did that night. The way she was carrying on, I think she took advantage of the open bar, too. She danced with Daddy, she danced with Mr. Richardson, she danced with Mother Richardson's brother Charles. My mother had a good time. Daddy cried again during the father and daughter dance. My heart almost burst watching mother and daddy share a slow dance. It's not that I had any doubt that my parents were still in love, it was rare that I got to witness their intimate moments. The night was magical. At least the first part of the evening.

Jonathan and I were heading out to Chicago the day after our wedding. There was no time for a formal honeymoon. We reserved a small guest cottage that sat by a small lake on the golf course that was part of the Elks Club property. The Elks Club owned five of the little cottages that they used whenever they were sponsoring out of town officials or an out of town member.

The whole night I knew the time was coming, but now that it had come, I was nervous and excited. My new husband was so drunk by the end of the night, it took Matt and his two friends, Tim and Raymond, to get him in the little cart that was used to drive across the property. The guys drove one cart and Jennifer and I followed them in another. I didn't have a clue on how to drive. Thank goodness Jen did. Jen and I talked non-stop about the ceremony, and how great our friends looked all dressed up. It almost felt like a second prom. It tickled us pink that we were able to have the reception at the "exclusive" Elks Club and how I would have access to it whenever I wanted. We planned on using it during one of our school breaks home to have lunch in the fancy dining room. We both laughed at the thought.

Jen said during the reception, she thought she saw Peggy sneaking off with this boy named Mike who played on the basketball team with Jonathan. That's when the topic of sex came up. We tried to figure out who in our class may have already done it. We both agreed Peggy had. All of a sudden Jennifer squealed out, "Oh my god Katie, you're actually getting ready to have sex!"

We both started to giggle, then laugh, and we couldn't stop laughing. I thought Jen was going to crash our cart, we laughed so much. But then suddenly, I found myself crying uncontrollably. I was crying so hard, I was shaking. I couldn't catch my breath. Jennifer pulled the cart over and stopped.

"Sweetheart, whatever is wrong?" Jen asked with concern. "Slow your breathing down. Put your head between your knees."

After a few seconds with my head down, my breathing slowly returned to normal.

"Jen, I'm scared to death. I knew this night was coming but I don't think I'm ready to do this!" I felt myself getting anxious. Jen grabbed both my hands.

"But, honey I don't understand, why? Don't you find Jonathan attractive?"

"Of course, I do!"

"Then for heaven's sake, what are you afraid of?"

I let go of Jennifer's hand to wipe the tears away from my face and search for a napkin or tissue to blow my runny nose. "The whole idea of how this is supposed to work. Jonathan and I, we never did anything inappropriate. I mean outside of heavy kissing. A few times I let him feel my boobs, but that was always on top of clothes, never under." I started to cry again.

Jennifer took a tissue out of her purse and handed to me. "Well, haven't you at least seen it, or felt it?" she asked.

"One time we were kissing and he got so excited I felt his, you know what, against my leg. Oh my god Jennifer, it's huge! There is no way this is going to work. I don't see how all of that is going to fit into me and feel any kind of good."

Jennifer looked at me a bit stunned. "Oh my, I see. Well didn't your mother explain to you what to expect?"

I let out a chuckle while blowing my nose. "My mother said the less a girl knows going into the marriage bed the better. Mother says that assures the man that you're a virgin. Mother says that if a girl knows too much about sex before she gets married, her husband will know she learned it from being with some other man."

"Oh my!" Jennifer was still looking at me both stunned and concerned. "Did she tell you anything you should do?"

My crying had calmed down and I was able to breathe more relaxed. "No, she just said all I need to do is lay down and Jonathan would know how to do everything else."

Sitting in that small cart, looking into Jennifer's face, I could tell she was just short of laughing out loud. But, she was my best friend in the whole wide world, so she didn't. We rode in silence the rest of the way to the cottage. She parked behind the boys' cart. As we pulled up, we saw the boys still struggling to get Jonathan out of the cart and into the cottage. While we sat there, Jen mapped out for me the fundamentals of sex. She educated me on what would happen and how I should expect it to feel.

After our talk, I was still a bit nervous, but not as hysterical. I had no idea she knew so much about what a woman's role in sex would be. I chalked it up to her having three older, married sisters. Girls do talk about things like that. I would assume sisters would talk even more. Thoughts of sisters cuddled together in one room sharing secrets and tips on life, made me wish I weren't an only child. I wished I had a few sisters to calm down and give the talk to on their wedding night the way Jen had done for me.

By the time the boys came outside, I had completely calmed down. The inevitable happenings of the night weren't quite so frightening. Jonathan's best friend, Matt, walked right up to me and gave me a big hug and a kiss on the cheek.

"Congrats again Katie! You make a pretty good-looking bride. Jonathan is a lucky man."

I gave him a big hug in return.

"Thank you, Matt." I had known Matt for as long as I knew Jen. At that moment, I felt like I would always know him. He was like the brother Jonathan never had, and that made him family. He held me tight during the hug, then pulled back and looked at me with an expression I had never seen on his face before. It was a combination of concern and knowing.

"I won't be able to see you guys off tomorrow. The family leaves for our summer trip to Florida in the morning, so let me get my goodbyes in now." He hugged me tight one more time." If you ever need any help handling the big guy, you call me."

"Okay Matt, but I'm sure I can handle Jonathan." I gave him a kiss on his cheek. Wanting to find a way to lighten the mood, I turned to Jennifer. We both squealed and hugged. "I'll see you tomorrow at my house to get the rest of my packing done, right?"

"Yes, around 8:30 am. I'll be there." Jen grabbed both my hands and got nose to nose with me. "You are going to be fine. I'll see you in the morning. I want details." She kissed my cheek one last time. They all loaded into one of the carts and drove off.

I stood at the threshold for a few seconds watching them disappear into the distance before walking myself into the quaint, little cottage. In all of my fantasies of this day, Jonathan would sweep me up in his arms and carry me into our honey room. But, I walked in the door and looked around. To my left was a small kitchen area with a two-burner stove and an icebox that only reached counter high. There was a cute round table with a basket of fruit and other goodies in it. Next to that a bucket filled with ice and a bottle of champagne and two glasses. To the right, the room opened up into a small sitting area. Two wing-back chairs and a tiny round stand that held a simple lamp were placed in front of a small fireplace. There was a small fire already going. The night was too hot for a fire, but it was very romantic. I ran my hand along the back of one of the wing-back chairs. They reminded me of the chairs in Mother Richardson's sitting room. They had a really pretty floral print fabric with one coordinating pillow sitting in the middle. Behind the sitting area was a double bed that had Jonathan's too large body draped across it. The guys had removed his shoes. They also removed his tuxedo jacket and laid it on the back of one of the wing-back chairs.

Looking at my now husband sleeping, I was a little relieved. I had time to take off my dress, and maybe even take a bath and. . . who was I kidding? I was glad to delay the inevitable happening. . . sex. Our overnight bags had been placed in the room earlier that day. I grabbed mine and walked past a knocked-out Jonathan on the bed into a small bathroom. Like the rest of the cottage, it was well decorated with plush white towels and scented soaps that looked like rose buds. Mother had asked if she could pack my bag for me. I had so much going on, I was glad to have one less thing to have to do. I placed the small suitcase on the counter by the sink. I opened it up to a wonderful smell of Chantilly perfume and lavender bath salts. A beautiful pink chiffon gown with matching robe were folded neatly on top. When I lifted the gown, there lay high heeled slippers that had what looked like satin and some kind of feathery fluff at the front. My goodness they must have been at least three inches high. I giggled a little to myself. Next to the slippers was a cashmere sweater set and a form fitting black pencil skirt with a matching black scarf. The scarf had on it a pattern of little pink lips that looked like they were throwing kisses and gold lipstick cases that had the lipstick the same color pink as the lips. I recognized the sweater set and skirt immediately. Mother and I saw it in a fashion magazine a few months back. I never wore anything form fitting or tight. Mother always said that kind of dress was for adult women. I looked under the carefully folded stack to find a pair of patent leather black flats. The same kind Jackie Kennedy wore. I picked up the shoes and heard something sliding around inside them. Wrapped in pale pink tissue was a round gold brooch that had in the center of it a miniature apple tree with five outstretched branches. There were five tiny heart shaped apples, one on each branch. Each held a tiny diamond chip in the center of it. The moment I unwrapped it, the tears welled up in my eyes. I knew exactly what this small little pendant meant to my mother. I had seen her take it out of her jewelry box and actually wear only on special occasions. Other times, she would take it out and just hold it in her hand.

My grandmother passed away from cancer when my mother was around five or six. Daddy said from the pictures he had seen of her, she was a beauty and I looked just like her. Mother was raised by her much older sister Sara, who was only sixteen herself at the time. Grandmother's family didn't come from money. Her husband died when mother was two. As a single mother raising two girls, she didn't have much in the way of valuables to leave them. She did, however, have these pieces of fine jewelry. My Aunt Sara got a string of fine pearls. My mother got the brooch. She adored that brooch. I would even dare say, she loved it more than all of the fine jewelry Daddy had bought her over the years. The thought of her giving it to me, on my wedding night, made that much more valuable to me as well. I wiped away the tears and went through the rest of items packed. They were the usual toiletries and underwear. I was putting some of the things back into the suitcase when I noticed hiding beneath the underwear was a note. It read:

> To my daughter who is now a wife,
> Not long ago, you were my little baby girl. I am so proud of the woman you have become in such a short period of time. I am happy and excited about the life journey you are about to take. Enjoy every minute of it.
> Love,
> Your Mother

I could feel the tears welling up again in my eyes. Trying to envision my stoic mother sitting down to write me this sweet, emotional letter, and giving me her prized piece of jewelry. Maybe it was just the total excitement of the day. Maybe I was just exhausted and overwhelmed, but I started crying and couldn't stop. I felt alone. I missed my mother. I missed my room. I missed my daddy and the smell of his rum and coke. What was I doing here? I was alone in a bathroom with my drunk, passed out new husband in the next room. It was my wedding night and all I wanted to do at that moment was go home. I sat on the edge of the bath tub for I don't know how long and just boo-hoo'ed like a baby. I decided to run myself a bath using the bath salts from my suitcase. I needed to relax. I took my time allowing the water to calm me. Afterward, I scented every inch of my body with the Chantilly oil and powder that Mother had packed. I put on my chiffon gown and stumbled out of the room in my three-inch satin slippers, trying to do my best Marilyn Monroe walk.

Jonathan was still passed out; snoring loudly. I sat on the edge of the bed and kicked off the slippers. I tried poking him and holding his nose to possibly wake him up, but nothing worked. He was out. I looked past him and noticed the basket filled with goodies sitting on the table. I walked into the small kitchen to rummage through the generous stash. I retrieved a bottle of orange juice and a box of chocolates. I sat in one of the chairs in front of the fireplace. The fire had gone out. The chair sat close to the window that had a picturesque view of the lake which sat on the golf course.

It was a hot night, but the window was open allowing a soft breeze into the room. I sat there with my feet tucked under me, staring out the window, eating chocolates and sipping orange juice out of a champagne flute for what seemed like all night. Part of me sort of felt relieved that the whole wedding night ritual didn't have to take place right then and there. Another part of me was disappointed that this was how my wedding night was turning out; Me, alone, eating chocolates, sipping orange juice out of a champagne glass. I was supposed to be having sex. To think I had gotten myself all prepared to go through with it. Now that I knew all the details of what was going to happen, I wasn't as worried about it working out. The truth of the matter was somehow he was going to push his manhood into my womanhood, and something about that was supposed to be pleasurable. I didn't see how pleasure had anything to do with that. I wasn't looking forward to it at all! But, I was his wife and it was part of what wives did with their husbands. My head was lost in those thoughts, somewhere between the chocolates, the sky, and the orange juice, I must have fallen asleep. I woke up to the bright Georgia sun peeking through the window, and the sound of Jonathan throwing up in the bathroom.

CHAPTER 12

Jonathan
(The Last Day Home)

Jonathan couldn't remember how he ended up in the room, just that he was now in a way too small bathroom throwing up everything he had consumed the night before. His head felt like someone hit him from behind with a club. After about twenty minutes with his head in the toilet, he lifted it up to see Katherine standing in the doorway between the bathroom and the bed. *"Oh my god, she looks beautiful!"* He thought to himself. "Is there anything I can get for you?" Katherine said with concern.

As his new bride walked closer to him, he got a whiff of her sweet-smelling perfume and his stomach took another flip, sending his head back into the toilet. Five minutes later Jonathan came out of the bathroom holding a wet towel to the back of his neck. "Oh my god. I feel like shit!"

"Well I must say, you don't look much better than that either." Katherine replied with a soft chuckle. Katherine ran her fingers through Jonathan's sweat soaked hair. He was able to get a look at her for the first time since the reception. She had on a beautiful pink gown that hugged all the parts of her body that he loved. Katherine always reminded him of Jane Russell. Miss Russell was Jonathan's ideal woman. Dark and sultry, head strong and smart, just like his Katherine. His wife. He started to get aroused, as the thoughts of Katherine's body played in his head. It made him feel embarrassed and exposed, which in turn made him uncomfortable and upset. Why was she wearing something like that? Did they have sex last night, and he just didn't remember? That upset him even more, because he had been looking forward to being with her even more than the wedding. Katherine had been the source of all his fantasies ever since junior high when he first started to have them.

Too ashamed to ask, his mood went from embarrassed to angry. "Why are you still dressed in that getup?" He snorted. "Don't we have to get out of here? Don't you still have stuff at your house to finish packing?!"

Katherine was a little startled by her husband's reaction. "Don't you think I look pretty?"

"We don't have time for pretty right now!" He barked.

Keeping her head down she walked toward the bathroom. "It will only take me a few minutes to change. Maybe you should start loading up the cart."

He could hear the hurt in her voice as she walked away. Why didn't he just tell her that she was now, and had always been, the most beautiful girl in the world to him? Why didn't he tell her that he still couldn't believe how lucky he was that she agreed to marry him? How thrilled he was to know that she is now his wife. But instead of saying any of those things, he went about the business of loading up the cart that sat right outside their door. By the time he was done, Katherine had come out of the bathroom completely dressed. She wore a tight black skirt and a form fitting sweater that showed off the roundness of her hips and fullness of her breasts. Jonathan couldn't stop staring at her. Her hair was tied up in a ponytail with a black scarf and it looked like she had a bit of pink on her lips. As she stood at the door giving the room a once over, Jonathan thought she no longer looked like that high school girl he would follow around like a love-sick puppy. She looked. . . . like a woman. And she was his wife. They must have had sex. His best friend Matt told him that a girl always looked more womanly after she had sex. He only wished that he could remember it.

After he dropped Katherine off at her parents' house, he went home to finish gathering his things. He was both nervous and excited about starting his new life in Chicago. Packing would be easy. Besides his clothes, there was nothing from his father's house he wanted in his new home with

Katherine. He told no one he would be leaving early morning. He wanted to avoid the sad goodbyes. His knew his mother would be attending church and his father would be in his room sleeping in. Sundays were the only days his father allowed himself to sleep late. Most Sundays he would not emerge from his room until well after twelve o'clock. The staff always had Sundays off, unless there was a party or some other event planned. Jonathan slowly walked around the large empty rooms one last time. He made a promise to himself that he would never return to those rooms again. Walking into the room of his childhood for the last time, he laid down on his bed and closed his eyes. He thought about his mother and sister. He knew he would miss his mother. She was always loving and patient with him. A man should always have a place in his heart for his mother. He had hoped to spend some time with his older sister, Julie Ann, before he left town. She must have gone to church with Mother. She had moved to New York for college and after graduation, she stayed. Now she only came home on some holidays. Glad that she did make it home to be a part of his wedding, he was sure she would never move back to this house or this small town. Maybe, he thought, he would visit her in New York now that he, too, would be living up north. That was the last thought he had before he drifted off to sleep.

MY FATHER'S SON

CHAPTER 13

Katherine
(Breakfast with Daddy)

I sat across from Daddy for our last Sunday morning as his baby girl. Mother had gone on to Sunday service like she always did, leaving me and daddy to fend for ourselves. Mother stopped requiring me to attend service with her after I reached high school. That's when Daddy and I would have our breakfast talks. Most of the time I would awaken to the smell of fresh coffee and Daddy's buttery grits and homemade buttermilk biscuits, with warm syrup. Sometimes he had bacon, sometimes smoked sausage. That morning I surprised him, and had breakfast waiting for him by the time he finally came into the kitchen. "Good morning, Daddy!" I said to his surprised face. I kissed him on the cheek and told him to have a seat at the table. I sat his plate down and poured him his cup of coffee, before fixing a plate for myself.

"Well now, I didn't expect to see you here until time to get you to the train station. Where is your dear husband?" Daddy said with a smirk as he took his first sip from his cup.

"Actually, he had to go home to finish packing. Jennifer is coming by in about an hour to help me finish up." We were both quiet for a few minutes as we stuffed our faces full of hot grits and syrupy biscuits.

"So how did everything go last night?" Daddy finally said, breaking the silence.

"I don't know if I'm meant for this marriage thing, Daddy."

"Don't tell me there is trouble in paradise already." Daddy said while putting another piece of biscuit in his mouth. "It's not too late to change your mind. I have friends down at the courthouse you know. We can forget this whole thing ever happened!" He started to laugh.

"Daddy, I'm serious! "

"I'm sorry baby girl. So, you don't want to be with him anymore. What happened?" He said still chuckling.

"It's not that I don't want to be with him. It's just that he is so moody. I can never figure out what kind of Jonathan I'm going to be dealing with. I wish he could be more like you."

Daddy got a concerned look on his face. He stopped chewing his food.

"Did something happen last night that I should know about?"

"No. . . . . That's part of the problem. Nothing happened at all last night. On my wedding night I sat up watching my new husband passed out drunk!" I knew this was the kind of thing I could talk to my Daddy about. He was always good at translating boy language to me. But then he did something I didn't expect him to do. He started laughing. He laughed so hard he was folded over. Then I started laughing.

"This is not funny Daddy. That was not how I thought my wedding night was going to be. And if that wasn't bad enough, this morning I woke up to the sound and the smell of him throwing up for an hour. Then he was grumpy with me as though I had something to do with it!"

Daddy wiped the tears from his eyes. Through chuckles he said "I'm sorry pumpkin. I don't mean to laugh at your pain. Your mother and I did notice how much he was drinking last night at the reception. I thought he was just nervous. You know, the wedding night is special for the guy, too. There is a lot of pressure on him to get it right." Daddy gave me a wink as he took a sip of coffee. Suddenly, I felt embarrassed and a little uncomfortable.

"I don't think I should be talking about this with you." I could feel my face getting warm and I knew I must have been a bright fuchsia. Just then, Mother walked through the door. She grabbed a cup from the cabinet, poured herself some coffee, and grabbed a biscuit before joining us at the table.

"I am surprised to see you here so early Katherine. Why

is your father laughing and what did I miss?" she asked while sitting down.

"Maybe you need to talk to your daughter about the way we men carry on." Daddy was still in the midst of laughing as he tried to get the words out.

"Why, whatever is your father talking about? And why are you here so early? Where is your husband? I just knew you two would still be wrapped around each other." Mother looked from my face to Daddy's shaking her head in confusion.

"This is where I leave the room." Daddy picked up his plate and headed toward the small room he used as an office. We heard the sound of the radio he kept on the shelf behind his desk blasting out some sports event. Mother examined my face for any clue as to what was going on.

The conversations always went a little different when I was talking to Mother. With Daddy, I could say anything, without having to filter how I said it. Daddy was very easy to talk to. Mother was very much the opposite of Daddy. I had to make sure I said things just right or she would shut down like an old rusty machine and refuse to hear anything more.

"Katherine, please tell me what is going on. Did something happen between you and Jonathan?" I let out a slow sigh. I didn't know how to begin to retell the story I just told Daddy without Mother getting turned off. But then, I thought about the kind letter she had left for me in my suitcase. Maybe, since I had gotten married she would see me more like a woman, a peer.

I took one deep breath, and then told Mother how the evening unfolded. Once I started talking everything just came pouring out. I told her about the conversation Jennifer and I had. I told her about Jonathan passing out, me falling asleep in the chair and my waking up to Jonathan's throwing up the next morning. I couldn't understand why his disposition was so bad. How he just dropped me off at my home while he went to his house to finish his packing alone. The whole time I was talking, Mother didn't say a word. She just sat listening and sipping on her cup of coffee.

"Mother, I don't know what I did or how to fix it. I will be boarding a train, leaving my hometown to go all the way to Chicago to start my new life as Mrs. Jonathan Richardson and I have yet to sleep with my husband. I don't want the first time I do, you know what, to be in a dorm room!" I could feel the tears building up in my eyes. Mother stood up from the table to grab a napkin from the counter. I dabbed my eyes and waited for Mother to give me wisdom. After all, she and my father had been married for almost twenty years.

"Well dear." she finally said, "What did you say to him once you two were alone in the room?"

"Mother I don't understand what you mean. I told you, Jonathan was passed out on the bed by the time I came into the room." I could tell my voice was starting to rise.

"Katherine, you cannot just sit in the car with your friends chit chatting anymore, now that you are married. Maybe if you had spent less time talking to that Jennifer about sex, and more time preparing yourself for your husband, you would have had sex by now. That girl gave you wrong advice. It is the responsibility of the wife to be available for her husband sexually. Knowing fancy tricks is not the way to make your husband trust you or keep him satisfied. That is not the way a married woman should behave. A married woman always puts her husband first. . ."

Mother continued her speech about the makings of a good wife. I had hoped for a more supportive reaction. But Mother truly believed that sex was for the enjoyment of the husband and the production of children. I sat quietly in my chair while she went on and on. I wondered how Daddy felt about Mother's ideas on sex. I was deep in that thought when the doorbell rang. Just in time. I needed a reason to leave the kitchen.

"Excuse me Mother, that is most likely to be Jennifer."

I jumped up out of my seat and was out of the room before Mother could say anything else. As soon as I opened the door, Jen grabbed me in a suffocating hug. We both jumped around screaming before we let each other go. When we finally settled down in my room in front of the last remaining open boxes on the floor, Jennifer asked the question I knew she was dying to know.

"So, how did your night go? Did you do all the stuff I told you to do? Was sex everything we thought it would be? Come on, spill it!" I wanted to burst out crying again. I wanted to tell my best friend all about my disappointing night, but after Mother's reaction, I thought I'd better not.

"Jennifer!!! I am a married woman now. We don't talk about what happens between husband wife in the bedroom!" Part of me truly believed that I should keep my marriage to myself, but mostly I was embarrassed. The last thing I wanted her to know was that Jonathan was drunk, passed out cold the whole night, couldn't do his husbandly duty.

"Come on Katherine, you have to tell me something!" Jen was not going to let me off the hook that easy.

"Well I'll just say, it was a long night. I don't even remember when I fell asleep." I could feel my face turning pink. We giggled and spent the rest of the morning into the early afternoon packing up my life in boxes. We didn't pack everything, only the things we thought I would need in Chicago until I came back for Christmas.

"I wonder if the fashion is the same up north as it is here?" Jennifer and I struggled to close the last packed trunk.

"Well if it isn't, that will be a good reason to squeeze in some up north shopping into our budget."

"So, does that mean you told Jonathan about the account your father set up for you?"

"No, he still doesn't know. I think I'll wait to tell him. Jonathan is so determined to make it out there on our own without any help from our parents. Daddy said the money would be there whenever I need it. So, until we need it, it will just be there."

We finished packing. The rest of the time we talked about how our lives would be changing. What kind of adults we would be, and how all of it would affect our lifelong friendship. California was a long way from Illinois. But, we felt like we could still make it work.

Jonathan came by with his beloved mustang to have it

locked up in Daddy's garage. I don't know why he didn't leave it in his family's, it was much bigger than ours. Daddy agreed to house it as long as he had the right to take it out once or twice a month, to keep the engine from locking up, of course. Jonathan brought only one trunk and one suitcase. He stacked it next to the three trunks and two suitcases I had. The trunks were to be delivered by freight. We were taking the suitcases with us on the train. I was also carrying a small lamp that Daddy had in his dorm, as well as a handmade quilt Mother had in her dorm room. Miss Josephine was driving us to the train station. Daddy said he had a meeting and wouldn't be available to do it. Daddy rarely had meetings on a Sunday. What I knew about my Daddy was how emotional he could be. I'm sure he didn't want to break down in such a public place. Mother wasn't very good with directions, especially in the area the train station was located. She would get nervous and turned around. Good thing the station was not that far from where Miss Josephine lived. She came out on her day off to give us a ride. She was indeed a special person.

While Daddy and Jonathan loaded up the car and talked about the delivery of the trunks, I walked around the only home I had known for the last time. I knew I would be back to visit of course, but it would be with my husband in tow, no longer Daddy's little girl. Something about that thought made me sad. Standing in the doorway of Daddy's office, I suddenly felt overwhelmed. It was good neither one of my parents were coming to the station to say goodbye. I was sure I would be a ball of tears the whole way there. I walked outside to see Miss Josephine instructing Daddy and Jonathan on how to get the suitcases into the back of her car. I loved the relationship between Miss Josephine and my husband. I always thought it was sweet. Daddy came up behind me and gave me a hug. "Your mother may not show it, but she is going to miss you like crazy." Daddy spun me around and looked me in my face before giving me another hug. That time tighter. "You call me if you need anything. No matter what it is or what time it is! Promise me!" Daddy didn't attempt to hide the tears welling up in his eyes.

"I promise Daddy."

"You are the best thing about my life. I am so very proud of you. If at any time this marriage thing gets to be too much for you or even if you just need a break, you head on back home you hear! Your room will always be waiting for you."

I wiped the tears from Daddy's face. "Yes, Daddy I know. But I'm sure me and Jonathan will be just fine. You take care of yourself. I won't be here to see to it you don't over indulge."

Jonathan stood a few feet away waiting while Daddy and I got our last hugs in. By then, Mother came out to the car. She surprised me with a hug and a kiss on my cheek. "You take care of yourself and that fine husband of yours." I thought I saw a tear in her eye.

"Katie, sweetheart, we have to get going if we are going to make our train." Jonathan gently touched my arm. I looked into my Mother's face and saw the love I knew I would miss.

"I will Mother." I said just before getting in the car.

MY FATHER'S SON

CHAPTER 14

Jonathan
(Time to Go)

Jonathan loaded up the one trunk and suitcase he decided to bring with him. His room filled to the brim with trophies and ribbons of all of his sports achievements would be left behind. Just before he got in his car to make the drive over to Katherine's house, it occurred to him. How was he going to get himself and his bride to the train station? Mr. Shelby was kind enough to allow him to park his car in his garage for safe keeping. His own father threatened to sell it if he left it taking up space in the family's large three-car garage. But, Mr. Shelby would not be driving them to the station. Something about having a meeting. So, Jonathan had to figure out how he would get himself and his bride where they needed to be. His first thought was his best man, Matt. He then remembered that Matt and his family had already headed out on their vacation early that morning. He walked into the kitchen and opened the refrigerator looking for something cold to drink. As he reached for the pitcher of sweet tea, he thought about Miss Josephine. Her number was on a list above the telephone in the kitchen. She answered after the second ring. "Good afternoon, Josephine. This is Jonathan. I need you to take me and Katie to the train station in about an hour."

"Of course, Mr. Jonathan, I will be there right away." Jonathan could hear the smile in her voice.

"No, not here. Just meet me at the Shelby house." Jonathan gave her the address. she agreed to meet him there within the hour. Pleased with himself, Jonathan set out to see his bride.

Jonathan arrived at the Shelby house and just sat in his car. He hadn't spoken to Katherine since the morning when he brought her home from the cottage. His head was still ringing from the evening's festivities. Bits and pieces of the night were slowly coming back to him, but he was struggling with putting the whole night together. He was clear, however on how he treated Katherine earlier that morning. He knew he had to make it up to her. While sitting in his car, he saw Mr. Shelby come out of the house to the driveway. He unlocked the garage door and swung it open. Jonathan watched as he moved lawn mowers and hand tools to one side of the two-car garage to make room for his mustang. After he watched Mr. Shelby work for a few minutes, Jonathan got out of the car to help. "Good afternoon Mr. Shelby. Let me give you a hand."

"Good afternoon to you, too. Thank you, I could use some help. " Mr. Shelby looked up to see Jonathan walking down his long driveway toward him. Both men got to work rearranging the garage to accommodate Jonathan's car. Jonathan backed his prize possession into the spot. It was a perfect fit. Mr. Shelby then covered the car with a thick blanket for safe keeping. Miss Josephine parked her car at the end of the driveway and walked up to the two men.

"Josephine, pull the car into the driveway so that we can put the suitcases in without having to walk all the way to the curb!" Jonathan bellowed out to her before she reached them.

"Yes sir, Mr. Jonathan." Josephine was about to turn around to do what she was told. Mr. Shelby ran down to meet her before she could reach her car. Jonathan watched as they greeted each other with a short hug. They had a small conversation at the curb before Mr. Shelby took the keys from Josephine and backed her car into the driveway himself. Josephine got into the car as Mr. Shelby got out. Katherine came outside with her best friend Jennifer. They each carried a suitcase. Katherine also had a lamp in her hand and what looked like a small quilt thrown across her arm.

"Good afternoon husband. I'm going to walk Jennifer to

her car." Katherine gave Jonathan a soft kiss on the cheek.

"Hello Jonathan. Congratulations again. You two have safe travels. I will see you during Christmas break." Jennifer gave Jonathan a short hug, then continued down the driveway with Katherine. He felt his body relax a bit. Katherine didn't seem to be upset with him about the morning. He watched her place her things in the back of Miss Josephine's car. He then followed Mr. Shelby into the house to get the rest of her things.

The men sat Katherine's two trunks right next to Jonathan's one trunk in front of the closed garage door. Miss Josephine had gotten out of the car to help them figure out how to fit the suitcases into her overcrowded trunk. Katherine came outside and stood watching. She had tears in her eyes. Mr. Shelby stopped what he was doing to give his daughter a hug. After getting the three suitcases successfully to the trunk, Jonathan stood a few feet away to allow the father daughter moment. How must that feel, he thought to himself, to have a father who openly shows you love and affection and comfort. That was a feeling foreign to him, but one he promised he would give his own children, just like he was watching Mr. Shelby do for his Katie. Not wanting to interrupt their special moment, Jonathan looked at his watch and softly walked over to them. "Sweetheart, we got to go now if we want to make our train."

"I'm ready." Katherine wiped away her tears and headed toward the car.

"Mr. Shelby, I want to thank you again for looking after my car. The way I figure it, anytime we come into town, we would stop here first. Besides, my father would forget to instruct Pete to turn the engine over every now and again. Shoot, he might even sell it. . . Ha-ha. So, thank you."

Jonathan extended his hand for Mr. Shelby to shake. Grabbing his hand tight, Mr. Shelby pulled Jonathan in close to him until he was whispering in his ear. "You make sure you take care of my baby girl. If I find out you aren't taking care of her, I will be on you like a tick on a dog's ass. Am I making myself clear young man?!" The whole time he spoke,

Mr. Shelby had a smile on his face.

Jonathan stepped back from his embrace. "Of course, sir. I want nothing but the best for Katherine. I love her sir. She is my wife."

"I'm glad to hear you say that son. We both want the same thing." Mr. Shelby gave Jonathan a hard pat on the back. He walked over to stand next to Mrs. Shelby, who was standing by the car, talking to Katherine. He leaned in to give Katherine one last kiss. Then he watched his baby girl drive away to start her new life.

CHAPTER 15

Katherine
(Our New Life)

The train ride from our small town to the big city of Chicago took almost two whole days. I spent at least half of the first day crying. I missed home so much. Well, part of it was for that reason. The rest was because I was scared out of my mind. I didn't know what I was going into, or if Jonathan and I would have what we needed to handle whatever it was. Jonathan and I had a strangeness between us and we weren't really talking. We sat across from each other with very little sound between us, just the sound of me crying. After a while, Jonathan tried to reassure me that we had planned everything out just right. He was so sweet. He tried to list all the things we had done to get ready for our new life. We had secured an apartment styled dorm room that was exclusively for married couples. We had an appointment to meet with our financial aid advisor the morning we arrived on campus. We would get our keys to the apartment and plan out our budget. That should have calmed my nerves, but it didn't. Neither of us had ever been on our own before. Well, if you don't include the time I traveled with my junior class to see a play in Savannah. That was only overnight. This was to be at least four years of our lives. A lot could happen to a person in four years.

I sat by the window watching all that was familiar to me flash by until it got so dark I couldn't see anything. I must have fallen asleep in my seat, because I remember Jonathan tapping me to come to bed. We had one of those sleeper cabins. The space was so tight, Jonathan had to fold his 6-foot 4-inch frame almost in half. I don't recall either one of us got much sleep. But, it did give us the opportunity to talk. We talked in a way we never had before. For the first time we both talked about our parents. What we knew they expected of us and what we expected from ourselves. Jonathan told me for the first time what was really going on between him and his father. How much pressure his father had put on him to be more like the man he was, instead of the man Jonathan wanted to be. I told him about how important it was to me to prove my mother wrong. That not all men wanted a woman to be quiet and just pretty, that some men loved smart women. Jonathan told me he was one of those men. That he thought my brain was sexy and that was one of the things he loved about me the most. He knew we could never have gotten that far without my smarts leading the way.

We talked well into the night, holding each other tight in that small space, to keep from spilling out of it. The next day we were more playful and relaxed with each other. We were both looking forward to lying in a real bed and holding each other. The night before during our talk, I told Jonathan about how our wedding night ended. He was so drunk, he didn't know if we had made love and he just didn't remember, or not. After I told him what happened and how he behaved the next morning, he was so embarrassed and sorry. He promised to make it up to me our first night, in our first apartment together.

The rest of the train ride flew by. We arrived on campus early Tuesday morning. To our surprise, the offices were open and waiting for us. The counselor handed each of us what was left of our checks after housing and educational fees had been deducted. The housing cost was split between the two of us. The educational fees were a bit different. Jonathan being an athlete, had to cover the cost of his classes and books as well as the cost of his equipment and uniform. Because his schedule wouldn't allow him time between classes and practice to work, his scholarship had to also provide money for food and clothing each month. When the counselor told us all that was connected to his athletic scholarship, Jonathan beamed with pride. He was able to cover all of his college cost without any help from his father. All he had to do was maintain a C average, run track and play basketball, all of which he was eager to do. After our conversation the night before, I knew how important making it on his own talent was to him. Jonathan knew he would get no assistance from his father.

My money was a little different. Although I had a full academic scholarship, it only covered my educational and housing cost, and barely covered the cost of my textbooks. I was able to get a part-time job on campus working at the school newspaper. I knew I had the account Daddy insisted on setting up for me to help with the unexpected things that would come up. I tried to talk to Jonathan about accepting some help, but he wanted nothing to do with it. He felt like we would handle anything that we needed on our own. From that moment on, I kept any news about the actual account to myself.

We took our checks and our keys and headed over to our apartment with our few belongings. The apartment had a few pieces of furniture, including a small table with two chairs and a bed. We both laughed at how short it was. Poor Jonathan had his feet hanging over the end for a month before we could get one large enough to accommodate his height.

That first day was spent with each of us running around getting classes and books, finding our way from place to place on the large campus, meeting teachers and coaches and teammates. Figuring out schedules. By the end of the night, we both fell into bed exhausted. I woke up in the middle of the night. Jonathan was not in the bed with me. Tiptoeing out of the tiny bedroom into the main room, I found him sitting at the small table studying a history book. "Jonathan, come back to bed."

He looked up briefly, then looked back down at the opened book. "Katie, I'm going to have to work real hard to learn all this stuff. I have to be sure to keep my grades up or I can lose my scholarship." The look on his face was stressed.

"Baby, you will do just fine. I'm here, too. We both have to keep our grades up. Together, we can do this." I took his face in my hands and gave him a gentle kiss on the lips.

Jonathan kissed me back. At first, it was with the same sweetness I had kissed him. Then, his kisses got hard and he pressed himself against my body almost knocking the wind out of me. We both stopped and just looked at each other for a few minutes. "Katie, are you ok with us doing this?"

"Yes, I'm ok." I was nervous, but excited at the same time. Unlike the night of my wedding, I wanted to feel more of him. I liked the weight of his body pressed against mine, his hands climbing over my breast and sliding down to rest between my thighs. My back arched to the rhythm of his fingers and when he parted my legs with his knees and slowly entered me, I thought my body had left the planet. The feeling was out of this world magical. That night was everything I wanted my wedding night to be. We took our time, learning each other's bodies, finding out what caused that jump-out-of-your-chest feeling for each other. Classes weren't set to start for two more weeks. Jonathan and I spent that first week locked away in our tiny dorm room apartment having the honeymoon we both dreamed of.

Once school actually began, we had to try to figure out how to manage our time between classes, homework, practice and work. We were still learning how to live with each other with all of that happening. There were plenty of nights I fell into the toilet because he forgot to put the seat down. We argued over which side of the bed was off limits to the other, and whose responsibility it was to wake us up in time for class.

We shared our first Thanksgiving together in our apartment eating food from the cafeteria. We both agreed we would wait until Christmas break before we made our first visit home. When it came time to buy our tickets to go home for winter break, Jonathan didn't want to go. He said he wasn't ready to see his father yet. He insisted I go. Daddy had been calling since Thanksgiving to make sure I was coming. I didn't want to leave my new husband alone for the whole holidays, so I convinced him to at least spend Christmas and New Year with his sister in New York. He thought that was a good idea and she was excited to have him. When I went back home that first time, I took a plane. Daddy met me at the airport in Atlanta. The whole hour and a half ride was me talking about school and my teachers and my job at the newspaper.

"Married life agrees with you baby girl. You look happy." Daddy managed to get a few words in during my brief moment of silence.

"I am happy, Daddy." I know I must of have been smiling.

"So, the athlete is doing right by you? Is he doing his husbandly duties?" Daddy started to laugh.

"Daddy!!!" I started to laugh myself. "For your information, we are both handling our duties."

It felt good to be home. When I walked into my bedroom, everything was as I had left it. Mother walked into the room and hugged me, longer than I can ever remember her hugging me. I let go before she did. She cooked my favorite meal for dinner that night. For the next two weeks, I felt like I was back in high school again. Jennifer had come home the night before Christmas, but she had to leave the day after New Year's. On New Year's Eve, Jonathan and I said 'I love you' over the telephone. We wanted to be the last persons we talked to for 1967 and the first persons for 1968. I landed back in Chicago on January 4th. Daddy wasn't too happy about me leaving so soon. Classes weren't scheduled to start for another week. My husband and I wanted to spend some time together before we had to start back on the rollercoaster of classes, and work, and practice.

The first semester of college was great. I was looking forward to the second. I loved college life. It was everything I imagined it would be. I had become friends with several of the wives who lived on our floor in the dorms. We would sit in the laundry room and complain about our husbands while we folded clothes. Some of the girls were older than me, so they would give me tips on how to handle some of the professors, which were the hardest classes, and how to avoid them. English, math and history were challenging, but I did love a challenge in the classroom. It was sociology and civic studies class that opened up my mind and challenged me in ways I never would have expected.

Most of our discussions were about the civil rights movement. I had been aware of the civil rights commotion going on in some of the bigger cities surrounding our small town, but I had no real knowledge about the real plight of the Negro in society. I learned about Malcolm X and the Nation of Islam, and the impact his teachings and his recent death had on the many lives of the Negroes who embraced his message. We watched the many debates he had with journalists and scholars around the world, including one he had at Oxford. He always spoke with such poise and intelligence. I must admit, I was a bit frightened by the anger that seemed to resonate in some of his speeches. The more I read about his life and the life of the Negro, the more his anger seemed to be the only reaction the Negro would have.

Studying the non-violent movement of Dr. King brought up different emotions. I was fascinated by the young college kids, some as young as me, willing to protest for equal rights. I admired them for feeling so strongly about their position, that they were willing to allow themselves to be humiliated and abused. I read of them sitting at lunch counters and marching for many of the same rights I took for granted. I watched news reports of people being washed off the roads with high powered water hoses, or dogs being turned loose on them simply for wanting the right to go into a store or buy a house in a nice part of town. It made me wonder about the Negro men and women in my own home town. I never really interacted with Negro kids my age back home. We had a young housekeeper once, but she spoke to Daddy most of the time whenever she was in our house working.

There were no Negro couples in our dorm building. There were Negroes throughout the school. There were a few in my classes. There was one Negro girl named Olivia who was in several of my classes. She was also a freshman. She also worked at the newspaper. She and I became fast friends as we both tried to navigate our way through campus life.

I was always impressed by how quickly she would grasp new information and solve problems in class. I thought I was quick. No sooner did the professor ask a question, Olivia had the answer. I was a bit puzzled by some of the professors' reactions, especially my math teacher, Mr. Daily. Even if Olivia's hand was the only hand up, he would refuse to allow her to come to the board to work out a problem or to let her answer. It was almost like he was mad that she was so smart. This would cause me to think about my mother. There were plenty of times I knew the answer as well, but I wouldn't dare put my hand up. The sound of my mother's voice screamed through my head loud and clear. "There is no need to let everyone know how smart you are!" And "Let the boys answer the questions first. Stop showing off!"

Those were the phrases my mother said to me often. And even though she was many miles away, I still heard her voice chastising me, warning me to put my hand down and let the boys show off. I sat in awe of Olivia's willingness to force Professor Daily to see her. No matter how many times he would turn his head the other way, she would shoot her hand high in the air until he had to acknowledge her. I wondered what her mother must have told her about being a smart woman in a world of boys. What was the voice she had in her head? One day while we were walking from class, I asked her.

"How did you get to be so smart? Are all the women in your family smart like you?" As soon as I heard the words blurt off of my mouth, I wanted to pull them back. I was embarrassed for even thinking about it out loud. I didn't really know her background.

"All the women in my family went to college. My mother and all of my aunts. Even my grandmother went to nursing school." Olivia said without sounding bothered. "Education is a big deal in my family."

"What about your men folk?" I asked.

"My father was the first in his family to go to college. In fact, my parents met in college, at a dance. My father works as an administrator for the city of Baltimore and my mother is an administrator for the Baltimore public school district. Yes, education is a must in my household."

"So why are you out here in Chicago by yourself? Why didn't you go to school closer to home?" The words just popped out of my mouth before I could stop them. Maybe this was none of my business. Olivia calmly looked at me as though she could read my thoughts.

"My family is very close. I'm not complaining about that. I'm sure that's why I have so much confidence. We support each other no matter what it is. That's a good thing. At the same time, it can be very suffocating. Everyone has an opinion on all of the decisions you get to make for your life. I want to be a reporter and a writer. I want to write for a major newspaper. My folks want me to be a teacher, or a secretary, or a nurse. All great and noble occupations, just not what I want to do. So, here I am, on my own, making my own way, so I have the right to make my own decisions."

My respect for that remarkable girl skyrocketed in that moment. We were walking up to our math class, when I stopped at the door, to ask one last question.

"How do you get the nerves to be so bold? These professors treat you horribly!"

With a slight chuckle Olivia replied, "Momma always said if you know that you know, then you a fool not to tell it. And if you were wrong, well now you know that too." She was almost laughing out loud. "Those words still jump around in my head. While I'm sitting in class with the answer pressing against my brain, I can hear my momma's voice saying 'Put your hand up foolish girl. You know, you know the answer'!" We were both laughing as we entered the classroom. Her mother's voice sure sounded a lot different than mine. My new friend amazed me. I hoped I would one day get to meet her amazing family.

Olivia worked full time at the paper. I still don't know how she put in all those hours and still had every class assignment done on time. I was struggling working only part time.

"You might be surprised what you are capable of doing

when you have to." Olivia had an academic scholarship that covered her tuition and books, but not much else. She had to work to cover her housing, food and anything else she needed. She didn't live on campus, in the dorms. She stayed at a woman's boarding house in one of the Negro neighborhoods near the university. I had gone several times to study in the room she shared with two other Negro girls. One of the girls also went to the university. Her name was Rhonda. The other girl wasn't a student at all. I don't recall if I ever got her name. She worked in the city at a department store.

I would go on the days that Jonathan had late practice. I didn't like sitting in the dorm alone. I always told him where I was going, but I doubt if he heard me. Most of the time he was only half listening when I would talk to him about Olivia, my classes, and the goings on at the newspaper. I even told him about her roommates. He had gotten so focused on his track practices, I'm surprised he got any studying in himself. Every time I would offer to help him with a paper or study for a test, he would shoo me away. He'd say he and some of his teammates were working together and he didn't need my help.

One time, on a night that I knew Jonathan had a short practice, I thought it was time for my two favorite people to meet. So instead of going to Olivia's room to study, I invited her over to study at my place. I had bowls of chips and bottles of coke for us to snack on.

"Katherine, this place is so cute. I can't believe you guys have all this to yourselves."

I was pleased that she liked my place. For some reason, her opinion was important to me.

"I'm glad you like it. I can't wait for you to meet Jonathan. Actually, I can't wait for him to meet you. I talk about you all the time"

MY FATHER'S SON

CHAPTER 16

Jonathan
(They Do Things Different Here)

Jonathan arrived on the university campus with his young bride early Tuesday morning. After an intense meeting with the financial aid advisor about budgeting their money, and the counselor helping with class schedules and books, they were both exhausted by the time they got to their dorm room. They both meant to simply lie down for a few minutes. When Jonathan woke up to go the bathroom, the clock read 10:00pm. Coming out of the tiny bathroom and walking onto the what must have been the main room, Jonathan got a good look at the place for the first time. The whole apartment could have fit into any one of the large rooms of his childhood home. He walked to the makeshift kitchen past the small wooden table that held the old lamp that Katherine brought with her. It had been her father's when he was in college. Laying in the corner of the room on top of an unopened suitcase was a well-worn quilt that had belonged to her mother when she was in college too. Jonathan envied Katherine's relationship with her parents. During the train ride she had exposed just how much pressure her mother had always put on her to hide how smart she was so that she could just get married. He didn't see that to be all that bad a thing to have in a mother. All mothers wanted their daughters to get married. And now that they were married, that problem between them had been solved. Besides, Jonathan knew how smart Katherine was. That was one of the things he loved about her.

Unable to go back to sleep, he poured himself a tall glass of water into one of the only two glasses they had in the small kitchen. He sat down at the small round table that held the lamp and opened up one of his new textbooks. It was a history book. It looked like it was full of dates and hard facts. Suddenly Jonathan began to feel overwhelmed. He had to maintain a C average in order to be eligible to run track and play on the basketball team. Being eligible to play on the team was the only way he could keep his athletic scholarship. He was starting to get that strange tight feeling in his stomach.

Katherine walked into the room. She asked him to come back to bed. Jonathan told her how worried he was about his ability to keep up his grades. Katherine cradled his face in the palms of her soft hands. When he looked up from his book into her caring eyes, he could feel himself calming down. She told him not to worry. She told him they were in this together, then she gently kissed him on the lips, a kiss Jonathan had been waiting to receive for the last two days. He pulled her down on his lap and kissed her back. First it was equally gentle, but with each kiss it became more passionate. He felt himself becoming aroused, which almost scared him. He didn't want to rush her or press her to do anything. He wanted it to be right, when she wanted it as much as he did. He knew he had to make up for their wedding night, and he was willing to wait for her to tell him when that time was. The harder he kissed her, the harder she kissed him back.

"Are you ok with us doing this?" Jonathan sheepishly asked.

"Yes, I'm ok!" was Katherine's response.

Jonathan picked up his bride and carried her into their small bedroom. Her body lay before him like a banquet table he couldn't wait to dine on. He wanted to just look at her like this all night. He had dreamed what he thought her body would look like, what it would feel like, but nothing prepared him for just how perfect she was. She responded to every touch, every move. When he finally entered her for the first time, he had to talk to himself to keep from losing himself in her. Everything about school and his scholarship that had his stomach in a knot, just fell away. All Jonathan could see, smell, or think about was Katherine Richardson.

The young couple had a week before classes were scheduled to begin. They spent the whole of that week learning each other's bodies. The only time they left the room was to visit the cafeteria. At the end of the day, Jonathan would hold Katherine in his arms while she slept after another passionate love making session. She was so beautiful, he thought to himself. The past week of making love and sharing dreams convinced him he was right to make her his wife. Together they would create the kind of family he always wanted. Together they would show his father that he had what it took to be the kind of man to have a beautiful and successful life, without his father's help. Jonathan was excited for this journey to begin. With Katherine in his corner, he could do anything.

Once classes started, it took a few weeks for the couple to get into a routine. The stress of their new fast paced schedule, along with just learning how to live together, caused them to argue, a lot! From whose responsibility it was to wake them up for class, to who got in the bathroom first. Jonathan felt Katherine's wrath the many nights her bottom fell into the toilet when he hadn't put the seat back down or when the last of the milk they stored in their mini fridge was gone and she had none for her coffee. After a month of trial and error, they finally had a pretty good routine that got them up and out on time.

In addition to getting used to his classes, Jonathan had to learn how to balance his mandatory basketball practices, with homework and time for his wife. Most often, the time for the wife got pushed back on his list of things he was trying to do. His fears about the difficulty of his college curriculum had come true. He struggled. He had two of his required freshman classes with Katherine. She helped keep him up to date on assignments and studying for tests. But the classes that he had to go to alone were a nightmare. He had freshman math and English, both of which Katherine had tested out of and was taking a more advanced class. He had scored low on his last two math tests and was barely passing English. And that was because Katherine was all too happy to write his essays for him.

Basketball practice became his mental getaway, despite the uncomfortable number of colored boys he had to play with on the team. Back home, the only colored boys he came in contact with were from the all colored high school that his school played only twice a year. Jonathan never interacted with them directly face to face. They were now on the same team! The practice teams were broken down in groups; A team and B team. Most of the freshmen occupied the B team. Jonathan became angry once he discovered that the few freshmen on the A team were colored boys. *This would never have happened back home.* Jonathan thought to himself. *I would never play second string to no damn coloreds.*

None of the actual head coaches had attended any of the first few practices. They were run by the upperclassmen and assistant coaches. He immediately made friends with the boys who looked like him, only to find himself being ridiculed for having what was described as a "hick" accent. He let it blow over, thinking it was just freshmen ribbing. But, for the first time in his life he began to feel like the outsider.

The day came when the head coach came to one of the practices. It gave Jonathan a little hope. The coach was a short muscular man named Mr. Patrick Nelson. The team called him Coach Neal. Jonathan recognized him as one of the coaches that had come down to his school to recruit. Coach Neal introduced his training staff and the other assistant coaches. He broke the teams into smaller training squads. "Take a good look at your teammates. You are going to be together all season." Coach Neal bellowed loud enough to fill the auditorium. Each squad had seven boys. Jonathan's squad had four white, including himself and three coloreds. One of the colored boys looked real familiar, he just couldn't place where he had seen him before. The colored boys stayed to themselves most of the time. They only interacted with Jonathan and the others during drills. Joseph was one of the boys Jonathan had formed a fast friendship with. He was from a small town out of South Carolina. Joe, as Jonathan and the other teammates called him, reminded Jonathan of home.

Joe's accent wasn't as pronounced as Jonathan's and he didn't get teased nearly as much as Jonathan did. But Jonathan attached himself to Joe.

One day, as they gathered their things after practice, he asked Joe. "Hey Joe, what do you think about them colored boys being able to play on the A squad and Coach has good white boys stuck on the bench? Shoot, where I'm from this is just not done!"

"Well they do things a lot different up north," Joseph said while he put the remainder of his gear in his duffle bag.

"There is something about that tall one that seems familiar to me."

"Which one? In case you haven't noticed, all them boys is tall." Joe said with a small chuckle.

"That one in the middle, with the big hair." Jonathan lowered his voice and tried not to just point to the tallest Negro boy in the group.

"Oh, that there is Willis. You should recognize him. I hear he comes from your parts of town down there in Georgia." Joe threw his duffle bag over his shoulder and headed toward the gym.

Jonathan picked up his bag and ran to catch up to Joe. When they walked past the group of colored boys, Jonathan got in another closer look at the Willis boy. He racked his brain trying to figure out where he might have run into him before.

"I hear he's also on the track team. Ain't you on the track team, too?" Joe yelled over his shoulder at Jonathan.

"Yea, I am. I'm sure I'll have remembered who he is before then." The boys headed into the gym and to the showers.

Jonathan only had to take four academic classes. His sports program was considered a class and he got credit for it. He had math, english, history and a basic science class with a lab. He was barely surviving any of them. The History and Science class, he had with his wife. Sitting next to her day after day, he began to realize just how smart she really was. In the beginning, she would encourage him to put his hand up by slipping him the answer to a question. As the semester went on, Katherine was so into the class, she would simply shoot her hand up in the air, no longer thinking about whether or not Jonathan was able to answer the question. However, once they were home in their tiny place called home, she would always make sure that she did his assignment, as well as her own. The following day in class, Jonathan would be lost. Not knowing the material or understanding the answers to the questions. He began to resent how easy Katherine caught on to information. Every time she raised her hand made his stomach feel tight. He started thinking that others were judging him. How could someone so smart be with someone so dumb? No one ever said anything like that to him. In fact, everyone knew him as that cute boy on the basketball team. The "B" team. That didn't stop Jonathan from hearing his father's voice calling him a dumb jock.

One day while sitting in science lab conducting an experiment, a young blond curly haired girl came over to the station that Jonathan and Katherine were working. She was staring right at Jonathan when she asked if the solution they were using had a positive or negative charge. Jonathan looked down at the girl, then over to Katherine at a loss for what to say. Just then, Katherine tapped the girl on her elbow and asked her something about how she had prepared her setup for the experiment. Blond hair swirled around to face Katherine. They began to engage in a deep conversation that sounded like gibberish to Jonathan. They walked over to the blond-haired girl's workstation and continued their conversation. Jonathan just sat there not knowing what to do next. He excused himself to go the men's room. After relieving himself, he stood at the sink to wash his hands and just stared at himself in the mirror. "How could she do that to me?" he thought. "Why would she let me look like a fool in front of that girl? Why didn't she trust that maybe I knew the answer?" He slashed his face with water, pulled himself together and went back to class. Katherine was still talking with the blond-haired girl. They both looked up when he entered the room. Katherine gave the girl a slight hug and headed back over to him. As Katherine walked away, Jonathan overheard her tell her lab partner, a dark brunette with chubby cheeks, "We know who has the brains in that couple." Both girls laughed. Jonathan was embarrassed and angry.

"Sweetheart, after class why don't we go to the cafeteria to get some lunch? We have an hour before your next class and my having to go to work," she said. Katherine began to clean up their area and pack up her books.

"No. I have to meet the team at the gym before class" Jonathan's voice was short.

"I didn't know you had practice now. When did they schedule that?" Katherine tried to lighten the mood.

"I just found out in math class. Joe told me."

"Why didn't you tell me. I was so looking forward to us being able to sit together."

"Well I'm telling you now. I gotta go." Jonathan grabbed his books and headed toward the gym without saying another word. He spent the next hour in the gym alone, pumping weights, jumping rope, and shooting baskets. When he saw it was time to go to his English class, he just continued to shoot baskets. The gym was the only place where he felt whole. No one there to ask him science questions or judge his intelligence.

The days ran into weeks. Thanksgiving came and went. With finals coming up, they both agreed it would be better to wait until Christmas before going home. As the time to prepare for Christmas break grew near, Jonathan began to have dreams of sitting in his father's den, small in oversized wingback leather chairs. His father's angry voice surrounded his childlike body. In other dreams, he was frantically trapped in a giant maze, while his father laughed sinisterly at his inability to find his way out. He didn't want to go home. He wasn't going to go home.

At first, he tried to convince Katherine to stay on campus and they could celebrate their first Christmas as husband and wife alone together. But Katherine was excited about seeing her parents and sharing with them how much she loved college and the city of Chicago. He watched as his shy little Katherine bloomed on the college scene. She made friends in the dorms with the other wives. Her college professors loved her. He even caught her talking to some of the colored girls in the newsroom where she worked, like it was no big deal to have them working, so close to her. Yes, this was all going just great for her.

Katherine spoke to her parents every day. They didn't have a telephone in their apartment but each floor had what was called the phone closet. It had five phones on the wall with five chairs. Katherine would call her parents every day around the same time. Most of the time it was during Jonathan's practice time. Katherine hated being in the apartment by herself for too long. She would speak with her mother then her father for at least an hour. Jonathan came home just as she would be wrapping up the call. If he came to the apartment and she wasn't there, he knew exactly where to find her. Some nights she would study with some girl in her room off campus, some girl she seemed to talk about all the time. This girl, Jonathan couldn't remember her name, also worked with her at the newspaper. Jonathan didn't really pay attention to Katherine's ramblings. As long as she seemed to be happy, he was fine with her new friendships. They agreed that Katherine would make the first trip home, alone. Jonathan would spend Christmas with his sister Julie Ann in New York.

He arrived in New York on Christmas Eve. Seeing Julie Ann was nice, but Jonathan was overwhelmed by the busy fast pace of such a large city. He cut his visit short. Two days later, he was back in his small campus apartment alone. He missed his wife. He would spend his time trying to catch up on his class assignments. When he would become frustrated with his inability to understand something in the work, which was often, he would go back to the basketball court. There were more kids on campus than he had expected. His new pal, Joe, had gone home for the holiday, but there was always someone to eat with in the cafeteria. One of the guys from the team had a New Year's Eve party on their floor at the apartment dorms. At ten minutes till the new year, Jonathan sat in the phone room talking to Katherine. It felt great to hear her voice. They had agreed to be the last voice and the first voice each of them heard for the end of the old and beginning of the new year.

Katherine wouldn't be back until January 4th, so Jonathan took that time to meet with the counselor about his scholarship. He had received his grades and was in danger of being on academic probation. His counselor was an older woman named, Mrs. Higgins. She reminded him of every librarian he had ever seen. She had dark brown hair that she wore in a low bun. She wore thick, black framed glasses, and she smelt of butterscotch candy. " You are lucky you did very well in two classes, but your math scores are low. In your English class, your instructor says you do well with homework essays, but your test scores again, are low." While she talked, she would look over her glasses at him as if she thought he had answers to her comments. "With the help of the high B's in your history and an A in your Science class, your GPA is struggling to be a low C. Now Mr. Richardson, just what are we going to do to turn this around?" Mrs. Higgins removed her glasses and sat back in her chair keeping her gaze directly on Jonathan.

The next forty-five minutes were spent revising his schedule to make room for a math tutor and a study group. "As long as you stick to this schedule and apply yourself in these new classes, I'm sure you will be just fine. Remember, you must maintain a C average to be eligible to play on the team. If you're not eligible to play, you are off the team. If you are off the team, you lose your scholarship." Those were the last words Jonathan heard as he walked out of the counselor's office.

The new schedule gave Jonathan a bit more structure to his day. Because he picked his classes with his counselor without Katherine, they were not able to get into the same classes. Katherine thrived, Jonathan struggled. With each poor score on a test or homework assignment, his father's voice got louder and louder in his head. *"I told you, you were an idiot. You didn't have to go all the way to Chicago to find that out!"* He could smell the leather of his father's office, almost taste it.

In the beginning, the thought of his father gloating served to inspire him, to prove that voice wrong. He stayed up late working on papers. He made sure to go to every math tutoring date and utilized the study group for every upcoming test. In some cases, his efforts paid off. He received a B on his midterm math test and a good job on his sociology paper. As the semester went on, the pressure to do well increased.

The highlights of his college experience were still wrapped around sports. Basketball season was over. Jonathan was told he had an outstanding season by Coach Neal. In fact, coach was looking forward to seeing him improve for next season. He went into track full of confidence. Similar to track, they were separated into training teams. He had convinced his friend Joe, to try out for the team. They had been working out together getting Jonathan ready for the season. They both felt that Joe was pretty good and could make it on the few spots left for open tryouts. Joe made the team and was then on the same training team with Jonathan. Most of the freshmen were together paired with an upperclassman. Jonathan was relieved to be with a group of all-white runners. Although he was getting used to having to interact with coloreds, he didn't like it one bit.

At the end of practice one day, on his way to the gym, he thought about what little time he ever had to spend in the company of colored boys his own age. The colored staff at his parent's home was the only time he had direct contact with anyone colored. He remembered seeing the gardener Pete's sons every now and then whenever Pete had a really big project at the house to do - like that time they had to remove an old tree out of the front yard. But, he hadn't seen them in years. Pete had five sons. All of them much older than Jonathan. Most of them were already married. Three of them had moved away to some city in New York called Harlem. He remembered seeing that name when he was in New York visiting his sister.

Then of course, there was Josephine. She was the housekeeper and cook. Thinking about her brought an unexpected smile to his face. She had been there all of Jonathan's life. The whole time growing up, it was always Josephine's large bosom that he would bury his tears in. Her full lips would kiss his bruises and make everything okay. Whenever his parents were called upon to do an event or go out to dinner, it was only Josephine they would leave him and his sister with. The older he got, it was her laughter and smile that made him proud of his accomplishments. It was Josephine who encouraged him and Katherine on their way to start their college adventure. She warned them of the worldly ways of folks in the north. "Them big cities can change you in ways that ain't good fo' nothin!" she warned on the way to the train station that day. "I had a cousin, Leroy was his name. He moved up to Chicago lookin' for work, he say. Ain't nobody heard from him since." Jonathan could almost hear her voice. "Y'all be sure to hold onto each other tight. Don't let them big city habits pull ya apart. Watch who you make ya friends!"

Thinking about Josephine made him a little homesick, an emotion he rarely allowed himself to feel. Josephine dominated most of his childhood memories. All of a sudden it occurred to him, with all that she meant to him, he knew very little about her. He knew she had children. He recalled when he was maybe seven or eight, his mother being very upset because Josephine couldn't help her prepare for an important dinner party she was hosting because she was in labor. Mother was really upset about the girl Josephine had referred to step in while she was out. The girl couldn't cook any of the dishes his mother had requested. None of the girl's desserts could hold a finger to how Josephine made them. Mother had to be in the room every time the new girl did anything to be sure she was doing it right. By the time the party actually started, mother was exhausted. That girl never worked for mother again. Mother went through several girls before Josephine came back. Each day a new girl came that wasn't Josephine, made Mother even angrier.

One day while sitting at the kitchen table eating his lunch, Jonathan overheard his mother talking on the phone to one of her girlfriends. "These colored girls are getting lazier by the day." Mother said. "My grandmother would never have been as understanding and patient as I have been." The third girl in as many days was standing at the sink washing dishes at the time. Jonathan watched her look up from her task for a second and look back at his mother before going back to what she was there for. His mother never noticed. She just kept on complaining to her friend.

"My grandmother told me that nigger gals use to have a baby and get right back out in the fields the same day. I don't understand why Josephine requires three whole days off. I certainly hope she does not expect this to be the case every time she wants to up and have a baby!" Over the years Josephine did go on to have more babies. Jonathan didn't know how many children she had in all, or how old they would be. Missing her the way he was, made him wish he had taken the time to get to know more about her.

While deep in his own thoughts, he failed to see where he was walking. A small group of his colored teammates were on the grass by the track stretching out their legs. Jonathan almost tripped over one of them.

"Hey, watch where you're going!" It was the tall one named Willis. Jonathan snapped out of his thoughts just in time to avoid stepping on the group. He still couldn't figure out where he had seen this boy before. All he knew was he didn't like his cocky attitude. Jonathan decided he needed to put this boy in his place.

"Watch how you talkin' to me, boy. It was an accident!" Jonathan said with a little extra bass in his voice, to show he meant business.

"Watch who you callin boy, boy!" Willis had jumped up and was looking down at Jonathan. Willis was so much taller than Jonathan his eyes were looking at his neck. Willis had to be at least four inches taller than him. The quickness and aggressiveness of the move startled Jonathan in a way he wasn't used to. He was used to looking down on people. He wasn't used to people being as tall as he was, let alone having someone other than his father be taller. Willis was right in his face with anger in his eyes. Colored boys back home would have never dared behave this way. It made him feel nervous and embarrassed. He took a step back and turned to walk away. As he walked toward the gym, he saw in his peripheral vision, a group of older white teammates laughing and pointing at him. He forgot about taking a shower. Instead of heading to the gym, he headed home. He wanted out of the area as fast as possible. Those same old feelings of defensiveness and shame rushed to his chest. He was back home, that same little boy standing head down in front of his father. He hated that feeling. He hated the Willis boy for making him feel like that. In his head, his father had somehow followed him to Chicago, to the new life he was trying to create for himself. He had followed him in the form of this colored boy named Willis who was from his same home town. But he would not allow his father's representative to win.

Racing home to his little apartment as fast as he could, Jonathan couldn't wait to tell Katherine about the nerve of the colored boy, Willis. *"It's going to be a long four years here if this was how all of these boys acted up here."* He thought to himself. Suddenly, the words of Josephine ran through his mind. He wondered if this was what she meant when she talked about how different folks acted up north.

Maybe Katie knew who this Willis boy was from back home. He doubted she would know him by sight. Colored boys knew better than to be in the company of white girls. But, maybe she had heard his name before. He was supposed to be a top athlete. She may have seen his name on a list of kids going out of town to college. Katie was smart about things like names and dates. She only had to hear something once and it was burned into her brain. It was those kinds of skills that made Jonathan sure she would be a great writer and reporter at one of those fancy magazines or newspapers she was always reading. Maybe he would get this boy's full name next time he saw Joe.

Before he knew it, he was standing in front of his apartment door. He heard the sweet laughter of his Katie's voice. It made his heart soar to hear her laugh. He also heard the sound of another voice behind the door. Just then, he remembered she told him she was inviting one of her classmates over to study for an upcoming test. He was in awe of how easy it was for her to make friends in the dorms and in her classes. She was always telling him about one new friend after the other. Yes, his Katie was doing really well up here in Chicago. He had been real popular back home. Making friends was as easy as talking. Most kids knew who he was before he said one word. He wasn't finding as easy a time of it in this new place. He was sure he would get the hang of it soon.

Jonathan was beginning to feel some of the anger from the earlier event slowly slip away. He heard the girl's laughter again has he opened the door. Once he stepped inside his apartment, he felt like he had walked right into a brick wall. There Katherine sat at their small kitchen table with a colored girl, laughing and sharing jokes as if they were old friends. It took a few seconds for the girls to notice he had entered the room. Instantly, his mood had changed. Like a bull in a china shop, he saw the colored girl and saw red. His reaction was swift and mean.

"So, I see you hired a girl to clean up the place for us. That's a good idea. Hey gal, do you do laundry, too?" Jonathan said in a louder-than-necessary voice as he slammed the door behind him causing the girls to jump.

Katherine's face turned a bright, pinkish red. She wanted to salvage the situation and take some of the sting out of the awkward moment. She knew that Jonathan's only experience with Negroes were with the servants who cooked, cleaned, and maintained his yard. Race was not something that they spent time talking about. Katherine had no idea how he felt about the Negro kids they were now encountering in classrooms and other ways on campus. Maybe he hadn't realized how different life was here.

"Jonathan, this is my friend Olivia. She is not a cleaning lady. She goes to the university same as we do. Olivia also works at the newspaper with me." Katherine walked over to Jonathan and slowly guided him over to where Olivia was now standing next to her chair. "This is the Olivia I talk about all the time. I'm glad you two finally get to meet." Katherine tried to keep her voice light and upbeat.

"This girl works on the college newspaper? How good could the paper be if they have colored girls working on it?" Jonathan said with a stern stare down in Olivia's direction.

"Jonathan!" Katherine's voice elevated. Olivia gave Katherine a sympathetic look and started to collect her belongings.

"I'll see you in class tomorrow Kat. Nice meeting you Jonathan." Olivia walked past Jonathan without looking in his direction. Just before she got to the door Katherine asked her to wait. She walked her the rest of the way to the door apologizing for her husband's behavior. Olivia looked over Katherine's shoulder and saw Jonathan walking over to the door.

"Don't worry about it. I'll see you in class." Olivia walked out the door and Katherine closed it behind her. She turned around only to be pushed hard up against it.

"Don't you ever raise your voice to me in front of a nigger!" Jonathan's face was nose to nose with hers. The suddenness of the in-your-face confrontation both scared and shocked her. She had seen Jonathan angry like this before, but only once had he directed that anger towards her. That one time he did, he promised her he would never do it again. Here he was, with his face inches from hers. His hands pressed against the door on either side of her head. She was almost too scared to breathe. "I don't care 'bout you talkin' to them niggers in class, but you will not bring them to my home. Damn it Katie, you had that wench sitting at the same table I have to eat my meal on!" Jonathan was yelling. His closed fist hit the wall to punctuate his words. "Do. . . Not. . . Bring. . . Them. . . Into. . . my home!" He pushed Katherine aside and went out the door, leaving Katherine to slide down into a crying puddle on the floor. She asked herself, what just happened!

CHAPTER 17

Jonathan
(Hired to Help)

Jonathan walked from the dorms back to the gym. He decided to take that shower after all. There were a few guys hanging out lifting weights or throwing around the ball in the indoor basketball court. No one else was in the shower room. He stood under the water letting it flow over his hair and run down his back. As he lathered up his body, he replayed the scene with Katherine over and over in his head. Maybe he shouldn't have yelled at her like that, he thought. But a man should only have to tolerate so much in his own home. It was one thing to have to get used to how different the coloreds were up here, but he shouldn't have to deal with it in his own home. She just didn't understand where a man had to draw the line to have peace.

He recalled his parents talking about the Shelby household. His father felt like Mr. Shelby was weak and allowed his wife to run things. The Shelby's didn't even get a house girl until Mrs. Shelby had to go back to work. She had to help provide for the family, because Mr. Shelby wasn't able to bring in enough money as a salesman. Their girl only came two days a week. Katherine was not raised with colored folks around every day, the way he had been. Jonathan figured to himself, she was just not used to the way whites and coloreds were supposed to interact. In fact, it was his dear sweet Katie that wanted to invite colored kids to one of their high school dances. She was just a kind-hearted person who saw the good in everyone. That was one of the reasons he loved her.

Feeling calmer after his shower, Jonathan dried himself off and slid into a pair of sweatpants he had in his locker. He remembered, for the second time that day, the warning words of Josephine. 'Hold on tight to each other and be mindful how the city can change you'. He would not let that happen to him and his Katie. Since he had cooled off, he would go home and try to make up with his wife. He thought, to himself, he just needed to help guide her through the way people were in the big city. Everything would be fine.

As he was heading out of the gym, he passed the basketball court. He saw Joseph and a few of his teammates shooting ball.

"Hey Jonathan!" Joseph yelled across the court. " We need a third man to play. You want join in?"Jonathan looked at the clock on the wall above the net. He had only been gone for an hour.

"Sure, I could play at least one game." One game couldn't hurt. One game turned into three. The longer he played, the better he felt. He was playing so well that even some of the older boys came over to pat him on the back.

"Wow, you're really good." one of the boys said.

"Aren't you on the track team?" another older boy said. Jonathan recognized him as one of the boys who had been laughing at him earlier.

"Yea, I am." Jonathan stood tall feeling pretty good about having the older boys' approval.

"One more game?" That same older boy said.

"Sure, one more." Jonathan began to feel like everything would be just fine.

CHAPTER 18

Katherine
(Olivia)

I never invited poor Olivia back to my apartment after that embarrassing moment. After Jonathan went storming out, I sat on the floor, by the door. I don't recall how long. I kept playing the night back in my head over and over trying to see if there was anything I might have done to upset him. Maybe he had a bad practice. Maybe we were too loud and someone had complained to him as he was coming into the apartment. That would have made him embarrassed. One of the things I was quickly learning about my Jonathan was, he did not like to be embarrassed. He got really mean when he was embarrassed.

Most times he would just shout and storm out until he cooled off. That time was different though. He had gotten in my face and scared the Jesus out of me. He pushed me. He had promised me he would never scare me like that again. Memories at the water tower rushed my brain. I felt like I was reliving that nightmare all over again. Not knowing what else to do I just started to clean. Every room, every cabinet and drawer in our tiny apartment got cleaned, wiped or straightened.

Rather quickly, I ran out of things to clean and my husband hadn't come home yet. I wanted to call Daddy, but I had just finished bragging to him about how great everything was going for us. I couldn't turn around and start complaining about Jonathan's behavior. So, I just cleaned some more. The whole place smelled like Pine-Sol.

Jonathan came in just a few minutes before curfew. He said nothing about where he had been or what he had been doing. I didn't ask. He headed to the bathroom and took a shower. I went to bed. Neither one of us said "I'm sorry".

CHAPTER 19

Jonathan
(Color Coded)

Jonathan never had to run into that colored girl at the apartment after that horrible night. He and Katherine didn't talk about it again. The rest of the track season was great. The guys were slowly starting to warm up to him and he was beginning to feel more like part of the team. One day after a particularly hard practice, coach called him into his office. Jonathan was sure it was to congratulate him on a job well done. Some of the other guys had really struggled to get through the practice, but Jonathan went through it with ease. It seemed the afterhours he spent on the track or in the gym working out were paying off. Jonathan walked in to the office with a big smile on his face expecting to hear about his outstanding season.

"Have a seat son." The coach said with a serious tone that threw Jonathan off.

"So, we had a really hard run today. How'd I do?" Jonathan was only half joking with his question. The track coach was a tall lean man in his early forties. He had a full grey beard and head full of thick grey hair. Most of the time he had a very serious expression, and was rather quiet, leaving most of the loud talking to his assistant coaches.

"Son, how do you think your classes are going? Do you know what your grades are?"

Jonathan was not expecting to have that conversation with his coach. He had an appointment to meet with his counselor right after practice. He honestly didn't know what his grades looked like. He did know he had been working really hard to pass all of his classes.

"Well sir, I do have an appointment with Mrs. Higgins right after I meet with you. I guess I'll find out how I'm doing then." Jonathan tried to sound carefree. Like he wasn't worried at all.

"Well I hate to have to inform you of this before you have had an opportunity to speak with your counselor, but your name has appeared on my list of ineligible players due to academic probation." Coach sat back in his chair with his hand folded on top of his desk.

"Coach there must be some mistake. I'm sure I passed all my last classes." Jonathan was embarrassed. This was not the conversation he wanted to be having with his coach. "Coach I'm sure my meeting with Mrs. Higgins will straighten all of this out." Jonathan again trying to sound upbeat.

"Okay son." Coach stood up and extended his hand for Jonathan to shake. "You come back and let me know what your current academic status is and then we can make plans for your place on the team for next season."

"Yes sir, will do." Jonathan took coach's hand and looked him in the eyes as he gave it a firm shake.

Jonathan sat in the counselor's office for the 45 minutes until his scheduled time, watching the other students come in and out to visit the other counselors. There were several kids who would go to the receptionist desk and give her their names and their student I. D. She would give them a check in return. Jonathan saw Willis and a group of some other colored kids. They gave their names the same way he had seen the others do. Willis, too, received what looked like a check. Jonathan noticed the envelope he was used to getting his check in was a different color than the one Willis had received. After the small group had gone, Jonathan went up to the receptionist. She was a chubby undergrad with red hair, and a freckled face.

"Excuse me, sweetheart." Jonathan said using the most seductive grownup voice he could muster up.

"Why are those guys checks a different color than mine?"

It worked. The chubby cheeked red headed girl giggled while turning bright red.

"Our checks are color coded based on what type of financial aid the student is receiving. What's your name? I'll look you up."

Jonathan told her his full name in his newfound sexy voice. He leaned on the counter so that he would be a little closer to the long register list of names she was going through. They both saw his name at the same time. "Okay Mr. Richardson," the sheepish girl began.

"No, please call me Jonathan."

"Okay, Jonathan. Your checks are from an athletic scholarship. The students who just left have an academic scholarship." The chubby cheeked girl looked up to look Jonathan in the eyes and then quickly looked back down.

"How is that possible? Some of those guys are athletes. I know the tall guy, Willis something or other, he's on the track and basketball teams with me. " Jonathan was feeling confused. He leaned over to look at the list, to check to see if the girl may have read it wrong.

"That's actually not that unusual at all. Some athletes who meet our academic qualifications for funding would prefer to not have their scholarships tied to whether or not they play on a sports team. That way if they choose to no longer participate in the athletic program they do not lose their scholarship funding." No longer sounding shy, the chubby cheeked red head said very matter of fact like.

"Well what about all of the cost of the equipment and uniform fees?" Now he was just getting frustrated. "I had all of those costs deducted from my check before I even got it."

Chubby cheek red head girl was beginning to get frustrated with the number of questions Jonathan was asking. "The athlete would have to cover those costs themselves. It is not covered under an academic scholarship. Unless the university's sports program promised to cover those costs as part of their recruitment of the player. I guess that would depend on how badly the university wanted them on the team."

Jonathan had heard enough. While he struggled to keep his scholarship, the colored guys were sailing along worry free. He wanted to turn around and leave the room, but just then his name was called to meet with his counselor.

Jonathan sat in the chair opposite the woman with the thick glasses. She had his files open in front of her. She didn't look very pleased.

"So, Mr. Richardson, the grades for this semester are in. I have some good news and some bad news. Which would you like to hear first?" Mrs. Higgins did not have even a hint of a smile on her face.

"I guess I'll hear the good news first."

"Well you did manage to pass all of your classes this semester." She said looking at him over her thick glasses

"Wow, I knew there must have been some mistake. I knew I had to pass. I worked really hard!" Jonathan let out a loud sigh of relief. Whatever the bad news was, he felt like he could handle it.

"What is the bad news then?"

Mrs. Higgins started to read out loud his final grades. Four C's and one D.

"Unfortunately, that D is enough to put you on academic probation. that of course then makes you ineligible to play on any of our sports team. If you can't play. . . ."

Jonathan cut her off before she could finish the sentence.

"I know. . . . If I can't play I lose my money! Is there anything I can do to fix this?" Jonathan was starting to get a stomach ache.

"Actually Mr. Richardson, there is. If you go to summer session and do that D grade over to get a C or better, we might be able to salvage your sports career with us."

"I'll do it. Sign me up for the class now."

"Don't you want to talk this over with Mrs. Richardson?"

"I'm sure she would agree this is the best thing to do."

"Okay Mr. Richardson, we will see you this summer."

"Thank you. Thank you again for giving me this

chance."

Jonathan left Mrs. Higgins's office feeling like he just dodged a bullet. Now, how to have this conversation with Katherine. She was looking forward to going home for at least a month of the summer. Summer classes started a week after the semester ended. Plus, he would have to pay for the summer class out of his own pocket. Katherine was good with budgeting and saving money. Jonathan just had to find a way to let her know that the money she had saved to make the trip home was going to be needed to pay for his class. He was glad this first year was going to be over. . . soon.

MY FATHER'S SON

CHAPTER 20

Katherine
(The End of Our First Year)

Olivia did everything she could to make me feel better about the terrible incident with Jonathan in the apartment. I wanted her to know that he was really a sweet guy and he had just had a bad day. I was so sorry he took it out on her. Olivia said that we would never have to mention it again. And we didn't.

Jonathan met Olivia again one time when he picked me up from the newspaper, so we could have lunch. He had better manners that time, but he still didn't really take to her. After that, Olivia and I only studied at her place or the library on campus. Whenever we got together, we spent most of our time laughing and talking. We talked about everything. It felt good to be able to discuss politics, local and world affairs, or anything else that came up with no judgment. I never felt silly for asking or saying whatever came to mind. We both agreed that we must have been sisters in another lifetime. We were studying the possibilities of past lives in our anthropology class. Our friendship felt so natural. I am sure the only reason I made it my freshman year was because of her. Between class assignments, work and Jonathan, I think I would have lost my mind had it not been for her ever-ready-to listen ears, or her soft shoulders to cry on. Although she was one of the strongest women I had ever met, she had moments when I got to be there for her, too.

One time one of her roommates, the one who wasn't in school, ran off with Olivia's part of the rent money. Olivia had given it to her to pay the rent on her way to class. When she returned home that evening her other roommate said the girl had cleared out all of her stuff and had gone. Olivia was at her wits end. She had no Idea how she was going to come up with that kind of cash. It made me happy to be able to give her the money out of the money that daddy had been sending to the account he had set up for me. I didn't have to tell Jonathan. I told her she didn't have to pay me back. She had done so much for me, but over the months she did pay me back. We were there for each other. She was the sister I wish I had growing up. I told her everything. I told her stuff I hadn't told Jonathan. She knew about the college applications and how we ended up at Illinois State. I told her about my uneventful wedding night. We had a pretty good laugh over that. She knew everything about my relationship with Jonathan. All of the good and all of the not so good. We shared everything.

Olivia was the smartest person in our social studies class and she was my best friend. Which was a good thing because I needed her to explain to me what the civil rights movement was really all about, not just the serialized version the professor was trying to teach us in class, but the real stuff I saw on the evening news. I wanted to know how Black people really lived their lives. Olivia never sugar coated anything. She told me how black people were forbidden to go into certain stores or certain areas. If they were allowed to spend their money in some stores, they had to go through the back door. Black people were restricted from buying houses in certain neighborhoods, even if they could afford to live there. Black people were cheated out of their wages often times working harder and longer than their white co-workers. Learning this made me think of the folks back home, folks like Mr. Pete who was always working. I was sure the Richardsons would make sure he got his fair wage. It was also from Olivia I learned that Black people didn't want to be called Negro any more. They were Black or Afro-Americans now. It was with Olivia I could have real conversations about being black: the day-to-day struggles they went through in this country. Things I took for granted. Sometimes I would come out of the conversation feeling quite embarrassed to be white. I wondered why none of this stuff was apparent to me before.

Of course, our conversations weren't always so heavy. Most of the time we just talked about girl stuff, like fashion, the latest hair styles, our weight, our classes, our professors and our men. I found out she was dating a boy who was also on the basketball and track team like my Jonathan. His name was Willis Johnson. One day while we were eating lunch, I asked her, "How long have you been dating this fella?"

"We met just before Christmas break. We have been steady since spring semester. He and I have the same biology class."

"Willis Johnson, why does that name sound familiar to me?"

"It should. He comes from the same small town you and Jonathan come from. I'm surprised Jonathan hasn't mentioned him to you. Willis definitely mentions Jonathan."

"I'll ask him about it. You know, back home the races don't mix like they do up here. It wouldn't surprise me at all if Jonathan didn't know who Willis was."

Olivia stopped eating and looked at me puzzled. "But your town is so small. Less than ten thousand people. How do you avoid bumping into each other's lives?"

I swallowed a mouthful of tuna salad before answering her question. "You would be surprised at how easy it is to be in the same room with someone and not ever acknowledge each other's existence."

"You and Jonathan still not talking?"

"We are, but it's not the same as it used to be. He's always busy with classes and practice and I'm always busy with classes and work. It seems we never have time for each other. I know he's struggling with his classes, but he won't let me help him. We don't have any of the same classes this time. It's just harder to be together than we thought it would be." We both sat in silence eating the remainder of our lunches, lost in our own thoughts.

"You know, boys don't adjust to new situations as easily as we girls do." Olivia declared as we cleaned up our table.

"He's adjusting to college in a new city and marriage all at the same time. That's a lot for any man to do. I'm sure next year will be much better."

"I sure hope so."

Later on, that evening I gave some thought to what Olivia had said. Maybe she was right. I loved college life. I loved the city. I had new friends and a great job. Back home, my Jonathan had been "Mr. Sociable." Everyone knew who he was and everyone loved him. Here he was having a hard time making connections. He had one friend who was on the both teams with him, named Joseph. He came by the apartment once. He seemed like a nice guy. I met him again one time when I brought Jonathan some lunch during basketball practice. Jonathan got very upset that I had stopped by. That was something I did all the time back home. But Jonathan said the coach forbid girlfriends or wives to come to any of the practices. He said it was a distraction. I never brought lunch out to him again. Olivia said she brought Willis lunch during track practice all the time. When I asked Jonathan about it, he just got even more upset.

"Are you really going to believe what that colored girl says over me?" He said sounding hurt.

"The new term is Black or Afro-American and no sweetheart, it's just that. . ."

"I don't give a rat's ass what them jigaboo's want to call themselves. I can't believe my own wife would believe one of them over me. I don't know if coming up north was really a wise choice for us Katie. It's got you making friends with all kinds of strange folks. I must say, I don't think I like it." The timber in his voice sounded disappointed, hurt, and annoyed.

"It's fine Jonathan. Of course, I believe you. I was just asking is all."

I let it go and never brought it up again. I was really trying to do what Mother said and stopped asking so many questions. I did notice it made home life a little less stressful, but I felt like I couldn't share who I was with him anymore. I told Olivia what he said. She just shook her head.

"Look Kat, I know you love him, so I'm just going to leave it alone. I will say, your husband has something going on in his head that makes no sense to me."

"What part makes no sense to you?" I asked.

"The whole thing sounds like he just doesn't want you around his team mates and that makes no sense to me." I knew Olivia enough to know when to let something go.

We were sitting on her bed packing up the last of her things. She was moving out of the woman's boarding house and the room she shared. She was heading home for a few weeks before moving into her own small apartment and starting a summer internship at a popular black magazine based in Chicago.

"What's the name of this magazine you're going to be working at again? Will it take up your whole summer? Will we be able to hang out a little bit before fall classes begin?" I was missing my friend already.

"First of all, this little magazine just happens to be one of the premiere magazines in the Black community. I'm still pinching myself to be sure this internship is real. And it's paying. I'm going to work my butt off to save as much as I can so that I can still afford my new apartment even when I start back to school and have only the school newspaper money to live on. I will only be home for two weeks then straight back to Chicago to start working." I could hear the excitement in her voice. I was so happy and proud of her. This internship was much sought after. My friend had to compete with some very seasoned writers. It was only for six weeks, but it paid double what she was making at the school paper.

"Have you two decided if you are going to go home or stay on campus?" Olivia said, while taping up the last box. Jonathan and I had been having some pretty heated discussions about my going back home this summer. He felt we couldn't afford the trip after we had to pay for him to take a summer class out of our own money. I didn't want to tell him that daddy had already sent me the money for my ticket. I simply said that I had worked a lot of overtime to pay for it. We had a week before summer class was due to begin. I asked

Jonathan if he wanted to go home, for even that short time. He hadn't spent any time with his parents since he started school last fall. He insisted on staying on campus.

"I think I might be going home for a few weeks, I'm not sure yet. Jonathan is staying because he has to take a class over in summer school." I said.

Olivia stopped taping to look at me. "How bad are his grades?" she asked a bit concerned.

"You know, I am not really sure" I said. "Jonathan has been a bit hush-hush when it comes to his grades. I do know that he needs to take over one class to maybe get a higher grade that will improve his grade point average. We started out taking classes and studying together. Now we have no classes together and he belongs to a study group."

"Have you met anyone from this study group?" She said with a raised eyebrow.

"No, not yet. But if he can actually make enough friends to become part of a study group, I'm happy." We both started laughing. I could tell by the look on my dear friend's face that she wanted to say something else, but she didn't. We finished packing up her life into five neat boxes and took them to be stored in her landlord's garage. Olivia was paying a small fee to keep the boxes there for the two weeks she would be out in Baltimore with her family. When she returned, we would move her into her new place.

CHAPTER 21

Katherine
(My New Best Friend)

We had lunch at a small cafe near the bus station on the day she was to go home. It was a small eatery that served soul food and made box meals to carry with you on the bus ride to wherever you were headed. As was usual when I was with Olivia, I was the only white girl in the place. I came to be quite comfortable with that notion. It was far less troublesome for me than it was for her when she was the only black girl in my world. We ate smothered pork chops and collard greens, macaroni and cheese and the best cornbread I had ever had in my life. It was better than even Jonathan's cook Josephine's and that was saying a lot. Olivia ordered a box meal to take with her. A meatloaf sandwich with chips and a soda pop.

We sat on the bench outside and waited for her bus to pull up. We talked until the bus arrived and it was time for her to board. "So, are you going home to visit your folks or not?" Olivia asked while we waited in line for her to board the bus.

"I'm sure I will. I don't want to go if Jonathan isn't going, but, we will see." I gave her a long last hug.

"You know where I'll be. You do still have the telephone number to my parents' house? I have yours. If I don't hear from you during the time I'm at home, I will leave my information with your father so you can get in contact with me once I start working for the magazine." She looked at me once more. "I do hope I hear from you." She gave me a hard squeeze one more time.

I waved goodbye to my best friend until the bus pulled away.

MY FATHER'S SON

CHAPTER 22

Katherine and James

I put my cup of coffee down and looked James in the eyes. His soft brown eyes looked back at me filled with sympathy and understanding. "I should call my office to let them know I'm not coming in. I should take a sick day. My eye feels like it's closing and I won't be able to read a thing with it like this." I could hear the sadness in my own voice. Reliving those moments of my life made me feel vulnerable and naked.

"I'll take you to the back where you can make a phone call." James' voice was calm. Almost soft.

He stood up and for the second time that morning, I noticed just how large a man he was. Not fat at all, but stocky and solid. Those kinds of things go unnoticed when a man is sitting down. He held his hand out for me to take, which I did. His grip was gentle and firm at the same time. We went behind the counter into the kitchen area.

"James, are we allowed to go back here?" I asked.

"Don't worry, I know the owner." He smirked, then winked. James kept walking through the kitchen to a small hallway that broke off into three separate rooms. One looked like it was a storage room. It had boxes lined and stacked up against the walls. The other two were offices. James entered the larger of the two and went to sit behind a very large desk. He pointed to a soft cushioned chair that sat in front of the desk and told me to take a seat. He pushed a few buttons on a complicated looking phone system, then turned it around to face me.

"You should be able to call out now. I'll give you some privacy." He walked out of the room. It was while I was on the phone with my supervisor that I began to notice the pictures on the desk and all over the walls. They were of a much younger looking James with various women. Two of them were older and two were younger. One of the women looked like the very talented waitress whom I had seen earlier. All of the women had variations of the same face. In all of the pictures, James was smiling or laughing with someone like he had just told the funniest joke. I looked hard at one picture of James standing outside of the donut shop he had gone to this morning, posing with the same brown faced woman I saw him talking to behind the counter. A closer look at the picture showed them having the same sweet smile. I finished my call and continued looking at the pictures that filled the walls, when James walked back in. "Is everything okay?" he asked with some hesitancy.

"Yes, everything is fine. You take a lot of pictures."

"I like documenting important moments. This here is a picture of me with my sister Gertrude when we bought the donut shop." He pointed to the last picture, the one I was standing in front of. "And this one here is my mother and Aunt when they opened their childcare business. And this one here is my baby sister Glenda when we opened up this here restaurant. Yes, I like to document the moments." James smiled that big smile of his and sat himself down behind his desk.

"Wow, you have a lot you're juggling." I said as I sat back in the cushioned chair.

"Not really. My sisters, my mother and aunt, they do all the real work, the day-to-day business. I just come in and sign checks and pay bills. Make sure there are no holes in the place. The women are the hearts that keep all this running. I'm pretty spoiled that way." James began to chuckle. His chuckle caused me to chuckle too.

"So, from what you tell me, you had a lot you were juggling. New city, college, new husband. Tell me, how do you go from being two young kids in love and excited about your new lives to this lovely woman sitting in front of me with a black eye?" James was no longer smiling. He sat forward in his seat with his hands folded leaning on his desk.

I sat back in the soft cushioned chair and closed my eyes. No one knew this story besides my best friend Olivia. It actually felt good to open up and let it out with someone. James had been my bus driver for the past five years. I didn't know him, but I felt like I could trust him with my story.

"Do you mind if I have something to drink?" I asked.

"Sure, you can. I'll call my sister and have her bring something back here. What would you like?" James had reached for the phone and was ready to press the intercom.

I paused for a second, then replied, "I could really use a tall glass of sweet tea."

ACKNOWLEDGMENTS

I have had stories play in my head forever, for as long as I can remember being me. They were there in my head, these stories. They were only known to me; never shared, but always present. My first captive audience were my little munchkins who would listen during long car rides to pick daddy up from work. Bedtime stories would stretch into "to be continued". Night after night cuddled together, they lay still and let me ramble on about the happenings of people they have never met, but who's lives they had become quite familiar with. Thank you, babies.

I want to say thank you to Brother D'Black sitting in 5th Street Dicks. That day, you grabbed my notebook and invited me to the Anansi Writers workshop at World Stage. It forever changed the trajectory of my life. No longer were my characters held captive on pieces of paper and tattered notebooks. I had found a group of people who actually wanted to hear my stories. They encouraged me to tell them more and to write them down.

Thank you, Coney Williams, for convincing me that I indeed had a book in me and that CLI would help to discipline my pen. You were right. Thank you Hiram Sims for creating the outlet for me to get this discipline. I never would have done it on my own. (I like to believe I would, it just would have taken longer). Thank you Jaha Zainabu, for being the patient and listening and encouraging you that you are. To all my classmates who helped to drive the story forward, thank you.

I want to give a heartfelt thank you to Staci, for willingly reading through so many of my very rough drafts and dragging your poor husband, Steve, into the project. I owe you both a serious cocktail. Liz and Verona, and all the ladies at Macy's who were my sounding boards when I wasn't sure which direction I should go. Thank you!

To all who buy this book, come with me on this journey, with these people, who have a story that must be told. They just picked me to tell it.

ABOUT THE AUTHOR

Kooki's path to expression through the written word and poetry began at a young age. At the age of 4, her family moved from New York to Los Angeles on the heels of the Watts rebellion in 1965. A natural storyteller, Kooki wrote short stories and poetry since 2nd grade. Never sharing her gift with others, she collected her thoughts on anything she could get her hands on amassing a collection of index cards, napkins, notebooks and even the margins of books. The characters whose lives unfolded in her head fought for their stories to come out and be told. Some voices were more insistent than others to be heard.

Many years and notebooks later while sitting in the historic 5th Street Dick's Coffeehouse in Leimert, a chance encounter with a local poet, D Black, led to an invitation to a writer's workshop at the iconic "World Stage". It was there she was introduced to the world of spoken word. The rest. . . well you know how it goes. Kooki began sharing her poetry and short stories on stages across the country. From Los Angeles to Washington D. C. Where ever she can find an open mic, she gives voice to the stories that scream to be told.

www.ingramcontent.com/pod-product-compliance
Lightning Source LLC
Chambersburg PA
CBHW050408030726
47503CB00006B/2081